'I intend to look for another job.'

Luke stood up suddenly, his body like a savagely coiled spring. 'Why?' he gritted. 'Money, possibly?'

'No, it's not money.'

'Then what?' he barked. 'You've made a success of your work, therefore I had assumed that you must enjoy it.'

'Work? Oh, I love the work. Surely I don't have to spell out my reason for wanting to leave?'

'By all means *do* spell it out.'

'The fact is, we're oil and water.'

Dear Reader

Easter is upon us, and with it our thoughts turn to the meaning of Easter. For many, it's a time when Nature gives birth to all things, so what better way to begin a new season of love and romance than by reading some of the new authors whom we have recently introduced to our lists? Watch out for Helen Brooks, Jenny Cartwright, Liz Fielding, Sharon Kendrick and Catherine O'Connor—all of whom have books coming out this spring!

The Editor

Kate Kingston was born in Yorkshire but now lives in Nottinghamshire with her husband whom she met while serving with the forces in Egypt. She has a daughter and two grandchildren, and her interests include antiques, walking, travel, embroidery and history. Her ambition to write goes back almost to childhood, but a chance meeting with a stranger who predicted that her novels would one day be published gave her the will to actually get down to it.

A WARNING
OF MAGIC

BY
KATE KINGSTON

MILLS & BOON LIMITED
ETON HOUSE   18–24 PARADISE ROAD
RICHMOND   SURREY   TW9 1SR

*First published in Great Britain 1993
by Mills & Boon Limited*

© Kate Kingston 1993

*Australian copyright 1993
Philippine copyright 1993
This edition 1993*

ISBN 0 263 77978 5

*Set in 10 on 11½ pt Linotron Times
01-9304-55186*

*Typeset in Great Britain by Centracet, Cambridge
Made and printed in Great Britain*

CHAPTER ONE

MERRILL paused for a moment, wondering if she had come to the wrong address. The sober red brick exterior of the building and the newly painted green double doors had given no hint of the chaos inside. But the handsome brass plate had borne the legend 'Woodline Design', so this had to be the right place.

She glanced uncertainly around the large foyer. Electricians working on high step-ladders were hanging an elegant modern chandelier, there was a smell of fresh paint and sawdust, and against one wall rolls of polythene-wrapped carpeting gleamed in the thin March sunshine.

Merrill's dark eyebrows lifted a little; surely there ought to be a reception desk, and someone to attend to visitors? All she needed was someone to accept her cheque and issue a receipt, but there was no sign to point her in the direction of the accounts department, and the staff of Woodline Design were conspicuously absent.

After a moment she approached one of the step-ladders. 'Excuse me,' she began, tilting her head to look up. 'I say! Is there anyone around who——?' She stopped, turning quickly at the sound of brisk foot-steps, then she hurried across the foyer, high heels clicking on the shiny floor. 'Can you help me?' she called urgently. The man seemed to be in a desperate hurry, but he wasn't the only one, she thought doggedly.

He wheeled round, and dimly Merrill registered lean

5

height immaculate in dark blue; then, at closer range, a taut design of no-nonsense features, dark eyebrows drawn in impatience over a straight, imperious nose. A shaft of sunlight danced on the single white streak that ran through his thick black hair. But it was his eyes that compelled her gaze; between generous lashes they glowed with an amber back-light. It was like looking into the eyes of a lion. No office lackey, this! Rather, the king of the pride.

'Yes?' the word came peremptorily, then his face cleared. 'Oh, of course. . . Look, Miss——'

'Stanton,' Merrill supplied.

'Miss Stanton. Can you give me just a few moments? I'm called to the phone urgently. I'll be with you in——'

A door in the right-hand wall opened, and a curly blonde head looked out. 'Luke! For heaven's sake! Mike's calling from Florida and——'

'All right, Kate, I'm coming. Damn telephone. . . Oh, and Kate—get on to the engineers again, will you? Tell them I can't keep trekking to the other end of the building every time. . .'

Merrill didn't hear the rest as he hurried away, before half turning to fling over his shoulder, apparently as an afterthought, 'Three minutes, Miss Stanton, and I'll be with you.'

Disorganised was hardly the word! Merrill observed with a wry smile as the door closed behind him.

The electricians descended and moved their equipment, and a moment later two men came in and began unrolling the carpets. Obligingly Merrill moved out of their way, but not before she heard one of them say, 'We'd better get this right, and quickly, but no cutting corners. Mr Travis is a real——'

Merrill glanced at her watch. This Monday morning

she was intending to register with a secretarial agency; a temporary job would do while she looked for something more permanent. And then she must get down to flat-hunting. So, with her thoughts intent upon her programme for the day, she did not immediately connect the two names. Then they hit her like two separate blows. Her grey eyes widened, and she bit back an involuntary exclamation. Luke—and—*Travis*. Luke Travis: the name that had featured twice in her cousin Elise's diary, referred to afterwards, cryptically, simply as 'L'. So *this* was Luke Travis. . .the man with the golden eyes and the get-out-of-my-way-I-haven't-a-moment-to-spare stride? This was the man who, according to Elise's diary, had spent several weekends at her cottage!

Merrill bit her lip, fingering the envelope in her handbag containing the last of Elise's unpaid bills—for an elm chest, a beautiful piece of furniture bearing Woodline Design's distinctive label. Yes, of course! It made sense.

For a moment Merrill's grey eyes clouded; winding up Elise's affairs after her death had been a painful business, but there was no one else to do it. Once, just to know that Elise was a couple of hundred miles away, profitably painting, had given Merrill a sense of security, of belonging. Sometimes Elise would come up to London to spend a few days at Merrill's flat and together they visited galleries, and saw a show. Or Merrill came north to unwind on leisurely weekends at Bracken Cottage. Happy times. . . But they had finished with Elise's death, and now Merrill had come back to the Midlands city where she and Elise had grown up before they went their separate ways. Elise had blazed a talented trail to an art college four years before Merrill took up secretarial training.

Merrill's thoughts snapped back to the present. Luke Travis's idea of three minutes was far from precise, she thought, and she couldn't really afford to wait much longer. It would have been simpler to post the cheque.

Yet she couldn't bring herself to leave. The prospect of coming face to face with the man who had figured so prominently in Elise's diary before her accidental death was just too intriguing to pass up. *Accidental* death? That was the word that Merrill balked at. Was it credible that Elise should have a car accident that involved no other vehicle, no jay-walking pedestrian, no treacherous roads? It had happened in a quiet Nottinghamshire country lane. And Elise had been a crack driver.

Merrill thought back to an afternoon last summer spent lolling on the lawn of Bracken Cottage. Elise was, as she laughingly explained, between menfriends, and the conversation had got around to her hobby of car-rallying. 'I love it,' she had said in her husky drawl, her eyes glowing. 'And I'm good at it; it excites me.' She had moved, disturbing the loose red blouse to reveal the voluptuous swell of her breasts, and lifted her face to the sun. 'And part of it is the risk. After the insularity of my studio and the quietness here I suddenly find I need space, movement, *thrust*. . . I have to go for things, grab them when they're offered.'

Seven months later Elise's car, with her inside, had been found crumpled against a tree.

How *could* it have been simply an accident? Merrill asked herself again, going over the same painful ground. Yet—the alternative? Could Elise simply have decided to switch off? In view of her lust for life, her appetite simply for living?

Wasn't that equally unacceptable? Unless, of course, there was a powerful reason, a revelation that would explain Elise's frame of mind on that last day. That was the question that haunted Merrill with a nagging sense of something left unfinished, unsatisfactory. . .

She shook her head slightly, trying to clear her thoughts, but a tiny suspicion, the merest thread of possibility persisted: it just might be that the man whose initial scattered the pages of Elise's diary before abruptly ceasing, three weeks before her death, could have some bearing on the mystery. It was all conjecture of course, Merrill told herself sternly, and yet. . .?

But there was no time now to speculate on that rather sinister connection, for Luke Travis was coming towards her with his brisk, certain step. 'So sorry to have kept you,' he said urbanely. 'We'll go up to my office, shall we?' Less a question than a statement. He hardly paused in his stride as he led the way up two flights of stairs and, outwardly calm but instinctively wary, Merrill followed.

His office was a large, airy room at the top of the building. The walls were white, but the angles of the roof and the three dormer windows had been lined with cedarwood which lent the room a very faint, pleasant scent.

'I must apologise for keeping you waiting, Miss Stanton,' he said formally, indicating a chair and seating himself to face her across a big black desk. 'My telephone's on the blink, and we're revamping the reception area as you'll have gathered. It should have been completed over the weekend. So I suppose one could say that you've seen us at our worst, and anything else can only be an improvement.' He allowed himself a faint, impersonal smile, then he stood up. 'Coffee?'

'Well, I only——' Then Merrill stopped. Maybe over coffee she could learn something about Luke Travis. A little detective work might provide an answer to the riddle of Elise's death. And when Merrill explained to him that she was here to pay for Elise's Shaker-style chest Luke Travis's reaction might betray something. Strange that he should offer her coffee, but perhaps this was the way this firm did things in the interests of good customer relations. He was probably under the impression that she wanted to buy some furniture.

'Thank you,' she said demurely. 'I'd love some.'

He was watching her with a glint of amusement in those remarkable eyes. 'I was beginning to think that you'd lost your voice,' he remarked. 'White?'

'Yes, please. No sugar.' She watched him go over to the coffee-machine hissing on a cabinet near one of the windows, saw him deftly take cups and saucers from a cupboard. He seemed to do everything with economy and a certain understated style.

She glanced idly around. The pale, polished maplewood floor was strewn with a few vibrant kelim rugs. In an alcove a shelf displayed objects made in various woods; she recognised a rosewood apple, a walnut bottle, a limewood fir cone. Lovely things, she thought admiringly, tempting one to touch and hold them. A striking modern bronze horse occupied a low table. This room successfully combined the old and the new, betraying an appreciation of quality spiced with a stark, functional modernity.

'This is a very pleasant office,' she began conversationally as he handed her a cup and went round to the other side of the desk.

'We're a pleasant company to work for,' he said blandly. 'At least, *I* think so. Well, now, shall we get down to business? I'm pushed for time as you may have gathered. What experience have you had?'

Merrill choked on a sip. 'Experience?'

'Well, of course. I take it that you're not straight out

of college? Or have you been on a re-training scheme? How old are you, Miss Stanton?'

'I'm—twenty-three,' Merrill said faintly, 'but I don't really——'

'An unnecessary question, I agree.' He swept away her words. 'Age concerns me less than efficiency. I'm looking for more than a secretary, you understand. More of a personal assistant. I made that clear in the advertisement, I hope. I need someone who's prepared to follow me around, to think along my lines and, in time, to anticipate my needs. Someone resourceful, adaptable, versatile, unflappable. And, above all, someone who wants to become *involved*.' Briefly he elaborated on the post. Then he leaned back. 'What I'm *not* offering is an easy passage with an eye on the clock.'

Merrill put her cup down precisely, her mind racing. It was beginning to make sense and now she could see the reason behind his original greeting in the foyer, the machine-gun fire of seemingly irrelevant questions, the offer of coffee. She stifled a grin. A ball of fire he might be, but he'd made one big mistake!

She opened her bag to take out the envelope containing Elise's account and her own cheque. That would take the steam out of him! Then she stopped, her brain buzzing.

'You seem hesitant, Miss Stanton. Something wrong?' His eyes held a slightly impatient glint below his frown. 'Maybe you're having second thoughts? You think the post I'm offering is too demanding?'

'Well, I——'

'If you would prefer not to pursue the matter, just say so, and we won't waste any more of each other's time.' He placed strong, well-manicured hands on the desk in a gesture of finality.

Merrill's fingers closed over the bulkier envelope containing her curriculum vitae and references. She took it out and passed it across to him. 'I don't think,' she said evenly, 'that you'll find any mention of feebleness and clock-watching in these.'

She swallowed a sudden sense of panic. What on earth was she doing, going along with this? Burning her boats, perhaps? It wasn't purely coincidental that she happened to be carrying the details of previous work experience, for she'd expected that the secretarial agency might want to see them. Now it looked quite possible that she wouldn't need the services of an agency after all—that was, if Luke Travis offered her the job, and *if* she decided to accept.

Seeing him now in a different light, she studied him covertly as he read quickly through the typewritten sheets. Judged impartially, he was extremely attractive. But then, those few of Elise's men friends whom Merrill had met had all been charismatic in one way or another. But Luke Travis was something more. There was a power in him, a suppressed vigour that made everything he did one hundred per cent positive. That would have appealed greatly to Elise.

Working for him would be no picnic, Merrill conceded. It would probably be difficult, demanding, ambitious. But, if first impressions were anything to go by, one thing it would *not* be: boring.

Merrill's gaze lingered on his mouth. In repose it had a curve of sensuality, contradicting the hard, square jawline, and hinting that, in certain circumstances, it could be persuasive and—exciting? For one incredible moment, Merrill knew a stab of envy of Elise. She shivered suddenly.

'I see that your last post was in London.' Luke Travis glanced up. 'Might I ask why you left it?'

Short and to the point, Merrill thought. She could be equally succinct and say, simply, because of a man. Instead, she said coolly, 'I decided to come home. I was born near Nottingham.'

'I see. Attachments? Husband in the offing? Children?'

'None.' Her manner matched his in abruptness.

'Right. I asked purely because the job will involve some travel. You're not averse to that?' As Merrill shook her head he deftly folded the typed sheets, replaced them in the envelope and handed it to her. 'I'm impressed by your past performance. I'm prepared to offer you the job, Miss Stanton. I'm a man of quick decisions, and I always back my hunches. Think you can cope?'

'I'm quite sure that I can,' Merrill said. Something about him was beginning to needle her, challenging her to meet him on his own terms. And, besides, there was the business of Elise's death. Luke Travis wasn't the only one prepared to back his hunches, Merrill thought, a trifle grimly.

'We'll talk about salary, shall we?' He went on to name a figure, and took Merrill's silence as acceptance. 'And naturally,' he went on smoothly, 'you'll be on trial.' He studied her impassively for a moment. She had the feeling that at any second he might get up and walk around her, judging her from all angles in much the same manner as one assessed the points of a horse, and she lifted her chin, staring at him coolly. 'As,' he resumed silkily, 'I'm sure I shall be—on trial, I mean. But that's only fair, I suppose.' He paused, still watching her with impersonal interest. 'Well? Do you want the job?'

Deliberately Merrill hesitated. She wasn't going to let him see that she would jump at it, although not for the reasons he might suppose. She crossed her legs and said mildly, 'But surely you'll want to interview other applicants?'

'I don't think it's necessary,' he dismissed. 'The reason I advertised for applications in person was to avoid wasting time on preliminary letters, short-listing and so forth. My previous assistant left without notice due to domestic reasons, and I'd like to replace her without delay.'

'I understand,' Merrill murmured. Obviously Luke Travis was not the kind to let the grass grow under his feet.

He was looking at her with one eyebrow cocked. 'Well?' he said. 'I'm a man in a hurry, Miss Stanton. Yes or no?'

'Then—yes, Mr Travis. I'll take the job.'

'When can you start? Next week? Tomorrow? Now?'

'Next Monday,' Merrill said firmly, feeling that the ground was being swept from under her feet.

He stood up. 'I hoped you were going to say tomorrow; however, next week it is. That's settled, then.' He gave a tight smile. 'I must admit that I hadn't expected such a prompt response to my advertisement. By rights, Kate—my partner's secretary—should have been sitting at a desk in the foyer doing the initial vetting, but you beat us to it; you were very quick off the mark. A point in your favour, actually. By tomorrow the place will really have a look of "business as usual", and——'

He was interrupted by the buzz of the intercom. He leaned forward and flicked a switch, listening. 'Right, I'll be down in a moment,' he said. 'And Kate, the vacancy is now filled, but perhaps you'd better take names and addresses of any applicants just in case they're needed later.'

They won't be, Merrill thought, on her mettle now.

Luke flicked the switch again, then turned and said formally, 'Thank you, Miss Stanton. We seem to have everything tied up.' He strode to the door and opened it, standing aside to let her precede him. 'I think we'll get along tolerably well,' he added, 'providing you're not afraid of hard work.'

'I've had no complaints so far,' Merrill returned smoothly, and saw his lips twitch.

'Good. I warn you, you'll be putting all your resources to the test, working for me.'

'Yes, I rather gathered that, Mr Travis. I'm sure I shall be equal to the challenge, though.'

The twitch broadened fractionally into what might have been a smile on anyone else but on him was just a rearrangement of composed features. 'Right, then. Monday it is, and nine o'clock sharp, if you please.'

With her mind reeling, Merrill walked ahead of him down the stairs and out into the windy street. She felt as if she had taken an extremely exacting examination. How on earth had Elise managed to tolerate Luke Travis? Twenty minutes in his company had left Merrill feeling stretched and apprehensive.

It wasn't until she began her tour of the estate agents that she realised she had completely forgotten to settle Elise's outstanding account. Still, she would be able to sort that out on Monday when she would become part and parcel of prestigious Woodline Design, personal assistant to a man who, one way and another, filled her with a sense of disquiet.

CHAPTER TWO

By THREE o'clock Merrill had almost exhausted her list of city estate agents. As she sat over a pot of tea in a quiet café she reminded herself that it was really expecting too much to find a flat as quickly as she had landed a job. Idly she traced the pattern of the marble-topped table with a slender finger. Not that she had really found the job, she amended with an inner grimace; it was more a case of the job having found her.

Luke Travis's manner of interviewing had precluded her asking many questions about the work. He had carried her along on the groundswell of his own forceful personality, but now that the ride was over she had time to wonder if she'd done the right thing. Certainly her main reason for accepting the post had nothing to do with the actual work involved, but the hope that closer acquaintance with him might throw some light on Elise's baffling death. Merrill couldn't imagine quite how this would come about; nor would it bring Elise back, she thought sadly. But if only for her own personal satisfaction it had to be worth a try.

She turned back to her list, crossing off yet another possibility and frowning into space. After the recent upheaval of leaving her London flat it would be good to get settled in a place here in the town. Bracken Cottage, which had come to her on Elise's death, was all very well, but living out in one of the Sherwood Forest villages would have entailed long rush-hour drives twice a day, and already Merrill had gathered that Luke Travis wasn't the sort of man to take kindly to excuses about traffic-jams. She would have no trouble in finding a tenant for the cottage; already Simon Clifford, a neighbour, had approached her on behalf of an acquaintance of his who was looking for a place in the area.

By five o'clock, just as Merrill was about to call it a day, she was offered the lease on a small flat in a pleasant, tree-lined avenue. It called for a celebration—a double celebration, really, she decided. New job, new flat, and Max pushed safely, although still painfully, into her London past: the background where he belonged, she thought wryly.

Bracken Cottage on a spring evening was a pleasant place, but celebrating alone was a contradiction in terms, she decided, as she took a sip of wine and looked without interest at the food on her plate. Tonight, alone and quiet after the eventful day, the shadows seemed to hold ghosts of the past, and there was so much here to remind her that this had once been Elise's home.

Resolutely she tried to shake off the memories, but they persisted. She'd had to come here to clear up Elise's affairs, taking a week's holiday from her London job. It had been a harrowing time. She had felt that she was prying into Elise's life, but it had to be done. There were painting commissions which Elise had undertaken but which would never be fulfilled; people to write to; telephone calls to be made. At the time, picking her way through the fragments of Elise's life, going through diaries and personal papers, had seemed like snooping. And during that miserable week the wind soughing in the trees and flinging rain against the cottage windows had added to the conspiracy of misery.

And then, that over, back to London to learn that

Max—just when she needed him most—had transferred his affections elsewhere.

But there was absolutely no point in dwelling on that, she thought resolutely. Off with the old and on with the new! She poured herself another glass of wine, drank it quickly and went next door to tell Simon Clifford that Bracken Cottage was available for his friend.

Merrill's forebodings about working for Luke were fulfilled during the first morning. 'My previous assistant was very methodical,' he remarked, with the ghost of a lifted eyebrow as if to query Merrill's understanding of his subtlety. As she nodded he went on, 'Alison was a great one for desk diaries and pending files. You'll have no trouble in finding details of my engagements and future movements, including the papers I'll be needing for a trip to Bruges next month. Of course, you'll keep my desk diary strictly up-to-the-minute. And you'll note that I prefer the somewhat old-fashioned personal touch to high-tech methods. After all, we're an old established company.'

Merrill smiled. 'Perhaps you'd like me to develop a copperplate style of handwriting?' she murmured, then could have bitten off her tongue. What a puerile thing to say! But he made her nervous with—with his height, his sureness, his whole aura. . .

'Not at all.' His glance denigrated her feeble attempt at humour. He frowned at his watch. 'I have to go out for an hour or so; therefore I suggest that you acquaint yourself with the filing system and generally try to get the feel of the place. Alison soon learned my style. No doubt you will too, Miss Stanton. I was able to leave most of the correspondence to her, and that's the way I should like to continue. As I said, we're an old established company, but we're forward-looking and vigorous. Very necessary in these days. I trust you won't find that too daunting?'

Merrill squared slim shoulders and met his eyes with a level gaze. He was the boss, after all, but he was beginning to sound like a slave-driver. 'Daunting? I don't think so. I did hold down a responsible job in my last post,' she said. Which wasn't strictly true, at least not in Luke Travis's definition. Elderly, softly spoken Mr Crawford in that rather Dickensian office in the City was a far cry from this. But her self-esteem needed the prop of that little white lie.

'Did I say something amusing?' Luke's voice clipped into her thoughts.

'Oh, no. No.' Merrill opened a drawer at random, took out a file and feigned immediate interest in its contents.

'Right. I'll leave you to it.' Luke turned away. 'I should be back in an hour, then perhaps you'll bring your notebook into my office. I like to clear all the correspondence before lunch.'

Yes, sir, Merrill retorted silently. This morning Luke seemed even less human than he had at the interview when obviously she had caught him in an off moment. Daunting was a word he'd used, and today his manner was just that. He seemed quite capable of crushing someone weaker than himself, and mentally Merrill armoured herself to meet the challenge.

So her early impressions were confirmed. He was an exacting man to work for. Who says that London is more frantic than the provinces? she asked herself wryly, as she began to come to terms with the diversity of her work.

Her office, opening directly out of Luke's big room, was pleasantly decorated, modern and well lit, which was just as well, for Luke had spoken the truth: a nine-to-five job this certainly was not! The renovations downstairs now complete, the foyer offered an impressive welcome with its effective lighting and elegant seating and the flower arrangements supplied under contract by a local florist. Woodline Design did not rest on any past laurels; it was highly solvent and very successful, and it didn't take long for Merrill to discover that Luke was the driving force behind it, and that her initial impression of him as dynamic was something of an understatement.

After the first week he dropped the formal address. Before she had finished one job he would call through the open doorway, 'Merrill, come and take a look at this, will you?' And she would have to leave whatever she was doing to sit in with him while he briefed her on what he intended to do, and why. Occasionally he asked for her opinion but showed no particular reaction when she gave it, so that she had no way of knowing if he was completely satisfied with her grasp of the work. But as the days went on she found herself working with him more and more frequently, delegating the routine tasks to the general office on the ground floor.

Certainly, she reflected at the end of a long, tiring but satisfying day, she couldn't have found a job more calculated to keep her mind off the past. Luke's attitude towards her was strictly businesslike. He didn't see her as a woman, Merrill realised, but simply as a useful adjunct to his own position in the company. Buttoned up and locked in was how she described him to herself. But that was all to the good. She wasn't in the market for an office romance, much less with someone whose association with Elise raised questions to which, in time, Merrill hoped to find the answers.

* * *

Two days of warm spring weather opened the flowers of forsythia bushes in the neglected garden behind Merrill's flat, and she hummed as she cut long stems of the starry yellow blossom. Soon she would get down to work on the garden; it would be something to do at the weekends. What better way to put down roots, and what more suitable time than in the spring?

After she had arranged the flowers in the brown pottery jug which stood on her office windowsill, she put the rest in the black glass vase in Luke's room. She was lifting it into its accustomed place on the top of his bookcase when he came in. He paused, watching her, and for some indefinable reason she felt her face grow warm.

'Charming,' he commented. 'I don't think I've ever had a lady bring me flowers before.'

'Maybe you haven't met the right kind of lady,' Merrill murmured.

'Could be. So what's the occasion? Spring in the air?'

'Something like that,' Merrill answered. 'So why not bring a little of it into the office?'

'Why not indeed?'

She knew that his quizzical golden stare had taken in that blush. 'Anyway,' she went on practically, 'these were left after I'd taken my fill, so I thought you might as well have them.'

'Oh, dear, and I was thinking you'd brought them specially for me. Such ruthless honesty certainly cuts me down to size,' he said idly.

Merrill smiled. 'I find that hard to believe,' she remarked.

'You'd be surprised,' he murmured. 'Well, now, delightful as this *bandinage* is, I think we should get down to work. There's a long draft report I would like

you to do, by lunchtime if possible. Got your notebook? Let's get to it, then.'

Later the same morning Luke asked Merrill to list
the dates of some previous meetings with a particular
client, and Merrill, leafing through last year's desk
diary, came upon Elise's name and address. The entry
seemed to jump off the page, twisting her stomach
painfully. Unexpected, it was like a surprise confron-
tation, and for a moment she could only stare blindly
at the familiar name.

Then, driven almost against her will, she searched
the following pages, but there was only one more
mention of Elise.

She closed the book wearily. Naturally there was
only one more mention, she realised after a moment.
Elise's name would no doubt have been upgraded to
the slim personal pocket-diary which Luke carried. She
felt suddenly sickened, reminded of her real motive for
taking this job with Luke. And that faced her with a
course of action which, for some obscure reason,
seemed rather distasteful now.

As the weeks passed she became accustomed to
seeing Luke already at his desk when she arrived,
immaculately suited, his dark head, with that one
dramatic streak of white hair, perfectly groomed, his
long, square-tipped fingers idly toying with a gold
fountain-pen as he frowned over his mail. So one
morning when he appeared in tan whipcord trousers
and a big, husky Icelandic-knit sweater, he interpreted
her surprised glance by saying smoothly, 'Don't be
alarmed. I'm still me.' He paused significantly. 'Or
perhaps that's what does alarm you.'

'Oh, so you've noticed?' Merrill returned, wishing
that she weren't quite so transparent.

'Well, I warned you at the interview that I was no

easy option, didn't I?' he barked. Then his manner changed as he eyed her curiously. 'How are you liking the job? It's difficult to tell anything from that smooth Madonna face.'

Merrill glanced away, shuffling letters into a neat pile. It was the first time that he'd come anywhere near to making a personal remark, and she had already concluded that she didn't register with him as a person, only as his assistant, sexless and insignificant.

'Oh,' she said thoughtfully, 'I'm quite satisfied with my job. Talking of which, I'd better look into these two queries before I do anything else.' She stared down at the papers in her hand, not wanting to look at him. Dressed casually, he seemed to have assumed the personality of someone altogether warmer and more approachable, even human.

'And perhaps you'll deal with all my phone calls. I don't want to be disturbed unless it's absolutely necessary. Repeat: absolutely. I'll be at the drawing-board, hence the more comfortable gear.' He got up. 'I don't believe I've shown you my studio, have I? Come along, then.'

It was a small room, furnished sparsely with a drawing-board on a stand, a high stool and a plan-chest. A large north skylight lit the room harshly, so that Merrill saw more clearly the fan of lines at his temples. Saw, too, the tiny flecks and threads of topaz and hazel that made his eyes such a compelling and disturbing feature. She tried to imagine him with blue eyes, or brown—or even grey, like her own; but she couldn't.

'So,' he was saying, 'no interruptions today apart from a refill of coffee now and then. If you're in any doubt, see Mike Freeman.'

With an effort Merrill pulled herself together.

Uncomfortably aware of his closeness in the small room, of the breadth of shoulders beneath the casual beige and black and oatmeal wool, she moved to the wall, ostensibly to examine a framed drawing of a wine-cooler. She saw that it was a working diagram, precisely drawn, but decorative because of its delicate penmanship.

'One of your drawings?' she said.

He nodded. 'I like to keep my hand in.'

'It's very attractive. . .beautifully executed.' Strange things seemed to be happening to her voice, and her words came in a sort of confused mumble. 'I like to paint,' she murmured. 'In water-colours mostly.' What on earth had possessed her to volunteer that information? she wondered numbly. As if he could possibly be interested in his assistant's hobbies!

'Really? There's a good exhibition in town—until the end of the month, I believe,' he remarked carelessly.

For one unbelievable moment Merrill wondered if he was leading up to suggesting they go together. But why should he? Never, by look or gesture or word, had he given her the slightest justification for thinking that he might be interested in her as a person. 'I shall probably go,' she said hurriedly. 'That is if I can find the time.'

And that was a laugh, she reflected ironically. Once out of the office she had all the time in the world and no one to help fill it. But at least the white lie had got her out of her moment of confusion.

'There's something else you haven't seen,' Luke said, unlocking a door which led off the studio into a small gallery. 'Here we are—a testament to the work of Woodline Design since its inception, although it had a different title then.' He flung aside dust sheets to reveal a Regency breakfast table, a Victorian chiffonier, an Edwardian plant-stand, art-deco bookcase—each beautifully made and finished scaled-down models of the furniture in vogue during different periods. Enchanted, Merrill moved past the pieces, studying them, watching as Luke demonstrated the action of a tip-top table, a secret drawer.

'They're—exquisite,' she breathed.

'Yes, aren't they, and of absolutely first-class quality. But that's our business.'

'Ye-es. . .' There was something about the moment and the intimacy of the setting that was driving Merrill to a sharp crest of awareness. Those wool-clad shoulders looked immensely powerful, and Luke's stance as he leaned against the wall watching her reactions showed the strong torso, the lean curve of casually-clad flanks. His eyes seemed to have gathered more gold from somewhere. . . Her heart tripped unevenly, and she felt suffocated. She managed to wrench her gaze away, and with conscious deliberation drew the dust sheet over a fruitwood table. 'We've left the office empty,' she said in a matter-of-fact tone. 'Thanks for the show.'

'My pleasure. Oh, by the way,' Luke said, locking the door behind them, 'Bob Tilling in Accounts just happened to mention the other day that you had settled an invoice for a piece we made for a client in Sherwood Forest.'

Merrill stiffened. 'A client in Sherwood Forest.' Was that how he dismissed Elise? And why raise the subject now, just when she wanted to get back to her own office to quell the bewildering inner turbulence which had disturbed the past few minutes?

'Yes.' She managed a nod. 'For Elise Masters.'

'Right. The Shaker chest.' When Merrill didn't speak

he said shortly, 'Of course, far be it from me to pry into a client's financial arrangements, but it struck Bob as rather strange. Quite a coincidence, in fact. Is Elise a friend of yours?'

So Luke didn't even know that Elise was dead! But why should he? If Elise's diary was anything to go by, their affair had finished three weeks before her death. 'Our mothers were sisters,' Merrill said abruptly.

'I see.' He had turned away and was uncovering the drawing-board as if he had no further interest in the subject. Merrill stared at his back, but he seemed to have forgotten her presence.

I will get to the bottom of it, Merrill resolved. But there'll be a better moment than this. After all, Luke was still something of an unknown quantity, and she had to be sure of her ground when the right moment came, otherwise he would annihilate her.

The following evening Merrill was meticulously checking the proofs of a glossy brochure advertising the company's line in executive office furniture. At the end of a busy day, broken only by a brief snack lunch with Mike Freeman's secretary, Kate, Merrill was tired. The darkness had come early following dismal March weather, and, alone in the office, she jumped when she heard a noise in Luke's room. As her door began to open she grabbed for the telephone, then dropped the receiver as Luke appeared. 'Oh-h,' she breathed, her heart racing, 'it's only you.'

'In the flesh,' he supplied. 'Why? Who were you expecting?'

'No one. . . I mean. . . I was about to telephone the police. I thought that——'

'I was an intruder?' He leaned against the filing cabinet, his short, dark coat swinging open to reveal the grosgrain lapels of a dinner-jacket and the fine tucks of a white lawn shirt below a black bow-tie.

'Well, you could have been,' she said lamely, irritated by his amused manner.

'Hardly. There's a security guard downstairs, as you well know, and the place is stiff with alarm systems.' He moved to stand beside her. 'How's it going? And don't you think it's time you went home?'

'Correct me if I'm wrong,' Merrill said sweetly, 'but I was under the impression that this was a rush job.'

'Everything's a rush job,' he said suavely, 'but it's simply a question of priorities. I'm not a slave-driver.'

'No?' Merrill sent him a disbelieving glance.

'You don't believe me,' he said easily. 'Well, just to prove it, come along. Leave all that. I'll run you home. Where's *your* car, by the way?'

'Being serviced.' Merrill leaned back in the chair, suddenly overtaken by weariness. She cupped her hands over her eyes. 'Those dimensions,' she murmured. 'I find I have to keep double-checking.'

'That's because you're bushed,' he said. 'We'll wrap it up tomorrow, together.'

'Sounds too cosy for words,' Merrill murmured.

He looked at her sharply. 'Always the keen riposte,' he remarked. He turned to reach down her fleecy cream jacket from the stand in the corner and held it out for her. 'Well, come along. What are you waiting for?'

She covered her machine and stood up, reaching to take her jacket from him, but he held it up, and she slid her arms into the sleeves. Half turning to adjust the big collar, her cheek brushed the back of his hand. That second's contact touched off an alarming ripple inside her and she moved away quickly, seeking refuge in trivia. 'How did you know that I was still in the office?' she asked carelessly.

'Simple. You were here when I left, and then when I was passing I looked up and saw that your desk light was still on. Ready?'

His sleek black car slid quietly through the thinning evening traffic. 'Bromley Avenue, isn't it?' he said.

'Yes, please. How did you know?'

'I make a point of studying my employees' records,' he answered carelessly.

'Of course. Silly question, really.' Merrill turned to stare out of the window. She felt downright uncomfortable; there could be something poignantly intimate about sharing the half-darkness of a car with a man— particularly when a tape played some soft Neapolitan music—and more especially with a man of Luke's charisma. And no doubt she wasn't the first woman to realise that. He was probably meeting some woman tonight, and obviously taking her somewhere glamorous. Merrill tried to imagine what his partner would be like, but lack of knowledge blurred the picture. What *was* his type? Elise had found him attractive—— more than attractive, judging by the diary entries and the odd, mysterious little symbols that appeared against his initial, presumably denoting a magic known only to Elise and himself.

'Going somewhere special?' Merrill asked brightly, when the silence between them began to grow oppressive.

'Just a dinner.' He drew away smoothly from the traffic lights. 'I suppose you must miss the bright lights of London?' he said idly. 'Coming back and trying to pick up the threads can't be easy.'

Merrill gave him a quick sideways glance. She wondered how he saw her—that was, if he ever gave her a thought, apart from in her official capacity. Had she, perhaps, unwittingly revealed the loneliness of her present circumstances? The death of Elise, and Max's desertion—had they combined to give her a look of pathos? Heaven forbid! She had absolutely no intention of projecting an image of a single girl, friendless, lonely in a hometown that had changed, spending her evenings watching television between rinsing out her undies and washing her hair.

'How do you mean?' she asked innocently.

'Coming back isn't always a good thing,' he said. 'The people one expects to be still around have often scattered, and things are changed. Friends have moved on.'

'Oh, I haven't found it at all like that,' Merrill said airily, crossing her fingers beneath her handbag. 'I have as full a social life as I want, and this town isn't short of night spots. And a new job—particularly the one I have with you—well, let's just say that I'm not left with much empty space in my life.'

He slid a disturbing glance over her as if testing the truth of her vehemence. 'I warned you about the job,' he said evenly, 'but you jumped right in.' He paused for a moment as if to give his next words emphasis. 'Almost as if you were running away from something. Or,' he added, 'perhaps chasing something.'

Merrill stiffened. Was he perceptive after all? 'I don't follow. You were offering a job, and I took it. It saved me doing temporary work which I don't much care for.'

'Well, I hope that your mad social whirl leaves enough room for that trip to Bruges next week. Still, in your usual efficient manner, you'll have taken that into account when planning your engagement diary,' he said dismissively.

Merrill sat upright, staring at his profile. 'Bruges? You mean—*I'm* going to Bruges? With you?'

'Don't pretend you didn't expect it! It's there in the diary, isn't it? And for Pete's sake don't tell me you can't——'

'No. . . No.' Merrill blinked. 'It's just that. . .'

Just that she had assumed that the booking had been made for him and someone else. Mike Freeman, perhaps. She hadn't realised that *she'd* be involved. 'I must be slipping. It hadn't sunk in that you would want me to go with you.'

'Put rather more accurately,' he said smoothly, 'I *need* you to go with me—as my assistant.'

'Of course,' Merrill said stiffly. 'A rather loose choice of words on my part.'

'I pointed out that the job would involve some travel. You seemed quite amenable,' he reminded her brusquely.

'So you did, and so I am. I'm quite looking forward to it.' Merrill raised her wrist to peer at her watch. 'Heavens, is that the time?' She was reduced to saying something—anything—rather than at this moment contemplate a trip to Bruges with a man whose mere offer of a lift home had shattered her poise so completely.

'You're in a hurry?' His dark eyebrows lifted sardonically. 'Then I do hope your devotion to duty hasn't made you late for some pressing engagement,' he added suavely.

You couldn't really care less, Merrill thought. 'No, I shall manage it,' she said. After all, one could hardly describe an appointment with a can of paint and a roller as 'pressing'. With a bit of luck she'd get the remaining two walls of her living-room finished tonight.

As he dropped her outside her flat Merrill felt a

small hollow of apprehension open up in her stomach. True, Luke had mentioned at the interview that the job would involve travel, and she had welcomed the prospect then. But now, in her present jittery, restless mood, it seemed fraught with danger. Bruges—with Luke. . . Strictly business it might be, but even in the tightest schedule there were small gaps—moments that could foster an ongoing intimacy or become fraught with an antagonism which seemed to be growing between them. Either way, a couple of days spent with Luke in a strange country didn't augur well for her peace of mind. But if there was one thing the past weeks had taught her it was that work was an antidote to worry.

Carefully she put her grey office suit on its hanger, bundled up her hair on the top of her head and climbed into a paint-spattered jumpsuit, firmly resisting any further speculation about the trip.

CHAPTER THREE

SATURDAY came, a sudden day of summer in early spring. The small untidy garden at the back of Merrill's flat faced south, trapping the warmth between its old brick walls. Still clinging to the maxim that work, particularly physical labour, could eclipse mental turmoil, she had gone out, determined to wrest some kind of order from the chaos of neglect. She managed to give the would-be lawn a rough cut with an ancient mower she found in the outside store, and now she was tackling the border where already green shoots pierced the earth with promise.

She had already spent an hour weeding and was determined to uproot a particularly tough dandelion; then coffee, then the weekend shopping and then off to the sailing club where she had enrolled for a course of lessons in board-sailing. That, at least, should be fun, and how she needed a little light relief! But first that wretched dandelion.

She bent, scraped away some soil and with both hands grasped the top of the root and pulled. Then, with a jerk, plopped down in a heap, a rosette of green leaves held in her hands. 'Blast!' she said, then began to laugh as she scrambled up. She would drive over to Bracken Cottage this weekend and get some of the garden tools which she'd noted on the inventory. How could she expect to do a proper job without the right equipment?

She turned towards the house, then froze. Luke Travis was standing at the top of the short flight of stone steps that led down to the garden. And he was laughing. How attractive he was! That was her first spontaneous thought, and then, but what on earth was he doing here on a Saturday morning?

Merrill walked slowly towards him. She wished she didn't feel so—exposed in the yellow halter-top and tatty green shorts which had seen much better days. And although his eyes didn't seem to move the prickle of her skin sensed that he hadn't missed a thing, from the mass of dark hair which was now half-up and half-down, to the crazy oranges-and-lemons earrings which she'd clipped on because—well, just because it was Saturday and sunny, and because she had felt like it.

'Having problems?' he asked, as she joined him. 'And what bizarre jewellery. Is that what the best dressed gardener wears these days?'

'Problems? Yes, but nothing I can't handle, given a trowel,' she murmured, hoping that her casual shrug would negate the blush she felt spreading over her face. 'As for the jewellery—well, I thought a horticultural theme was relevant.'

His mouth still quirked in the aftermath of his laughter, and she wished that he would move away from the top step so that she could pass him.

'And your. . .outfit,' he said. 'Oh, very suitable. The colours, I mean,' he went on as she stiffened. 'Green and yellow—you could be just one more spring flower.'

'But I'm not.' She managed a breathless laugh. 'Merely a hot and frustrated gardener. But I'm sure you didn't come here to talk about my sartorial kinks. . .'

'No, I've been to the office, and I wanted to look at the projected sales figures for this quarter. Can't find them in your files. It's unlike your usual efficient self to lose something so important——'

'They're locked in my desk,' Merrill said tartly. 'I'm still working on them, waiting for some details from Mike. And the key to my desk is in my handbag. I'll get it for you, shall I?'

'No hurry,' he said laconically. 'And I apologise if I've interrupted your work.'

'Oh, you haven't really. I was about to make some coffee,' Merrill said, then could have bitten off her tongue as he said,

'Splendid. You know my weakness for it.'

She smothered a sigh. Weren't five days a week enough without having to cope with him on a Saturday, too?

'It's instant coffee,' she warned. 'Not your cup of tea at all.'

'My, but we are sharp this morning. And the instant stuff's fine; I'm adaptable. Shall I come in and help you to make it?' That half-smile still lingered, needling Merrill. No doubt he was getting a great deal of macho satisfaction at finding her at such a disadvantage.

'Oh, I think I can manage,' she said sweetly. 'The instructions are on the jar, you know.'

'Perhaps I should have said razor-sharp,' he murmured.

'As you intend staying a little while,' Merrill said bluntly, 'you'll find a couple of ancient deck-chairs in that store. . .' She escaped into the house and went through to her bedroom to put on a dress. Then she thrust it back into the wardrobe. To cover herself now would be like doing a striptease in reverse, and would only emphasis her uncomfortable consciousness of her bare flesh. Better carry off an embarrassing situation with as much panache as she could muster.

'Tell me,' she said, as she set down the tray between them, 'do you always go into the office on Saturdays? I mean, don't you ever allow yourself time off from your job?'

'Why? Are you working up to a proposition? Shame on you, Merrill.'

She flushed. 'No, I am not,' she said crossly. 'I was curious, I suppose. But the answer's not important. How did you know I was in the garden?'

'I rang the front bell. No answer. I couldn't see your car parked anywhere so assumed you must be out. However, I came round the side of the house as a last resort and, as you see, my initiative paid off.'

'Oh, I expect all the others are out,' Merrill said idly, 'and I garage my car further down the avenue. And here's the key to my desk,' she added as she drained her cup.

'And thus I'm dismissed. All right, I knew that my visit wouldn't be welcomed.'

Merrill flushed. 'Sorry if I seem rude, but——'

'I know. You're busy. You won't mind too much if I finish my coffee, though?' he said with heavy irony.

'Oh, please don't hurry on my account.'

'I won't. Do you enjoy gardening?'

'I'd enjoy it more if I had the tools. . .but yes, I do. My father was a landscape architect, and my mother ran a nursery. She specialised in old roses, you know, the ones with——'

'Enchanting or unpronounceable names.'

Merrill smiled. 'You know them?'

'Oh, I grow a mean rose or two myself,' he answered negligently. 'And where are the parents now?'

'They died.' Merrill bent to put her cup on the tray. Then, sensing that her manner was too abrupt for courtesy, added, 'They were killed in a traffic accident in France.' Elise's parents had been involved in that accident, too, and it was only after the two cousins lost their families that they became so close.

'I'm sorry,' Luke said softly. 'And that's an inadequate remark if ever there was one.'

'It's all anyone can say,' Merrill murmured. 'How about you? Or isn't the assistant permitted to ask her boss personal questions?'

One corner of his mouth tilted in a rare smile. 'What on earth gave you that idea?'

'You did,' Merrill said pertly.

'Both my parents are dead, but I have a stepmother and a half-brother, Rob. He's joining the firm, so you'll meet him. Right now he's away on a skiing holiday catching the last of the snow.' Luke put down his cup and stood up. He seemed taller than ever, and his manner had reverted to its office-hours formality. 'I won't take up any more of your time, then. Don't work too hard this weekend. Remember, we're off to Bruges on Tuesday.'

As if she could forget, although she tried her hardest!

On Monday Luke came into Merrill's office, frowning. 'Get me the Charlton file, will you? Something's come up. . . Looks as if I'm going to have to dash up to London today and try to sort it out. It'll be a long job——'

'But—the trip tomorrow?' Merrill protested as she handed him the file.

'I know, I know,' he said absently, leafing quickly through the papers. 'I'll take the afternoon train today and stay in London overnight. I'll try and fix a working dinner with Charlton and sort something out then. . . Book me a single room at my usual hotel, will you? And I'll meet you tomorrow at the Victoria Jetfoil terminal. You've got our tickets, hotel reservations in Bruges, and so on? Good. And you can bring along the schedules we'll need while we're there. I'm confident I can leave everything in your capable hands. . .'

Merrill could see that he was totally engrossed in his forthcoming meeting with Mr Charlton; one of the things she admired about him was his utter single-mindedness. But a moment later he called from his office, 'I won't be needing you all the time in Bruges, so pack some comfortable shoes; you'll be free to explore a little on your own.' He glanced up to where Merrill had come to stand in the doorway, an amused smile flickering across his sensual mouth, his eyes slightly mocking. 'As an artist, you'll enjoy the many museums, I'm sure. You can even see a Michelangelo sculpture. I shall look forward to hearing your considered opinion of such treasures.'

'I've never claimed to be an artist,' she said coolly, 'simply an amateur painter, and therefore you'd find my opinion very uninformed. . . So I'll meet you tomorrow at Victoria, then, and don't worry—I won't be late and everything will be in order. I can't help wondering, though, why someone as high-powered and pressurised as yourself didn't decide to fly to Bruges? It would have been much quicker.'

'For the simple reason,' he said absently, pushing papers into his briefcase, 'that Alison—your predecessor—was paranoid about flying. She made the bookings, and it didn't seem worthwhile changing them, especially as you already complain that you're overworked——'

'I've never complained,' Merrill objected.

'Besides,' he went on, ignoring her interruption, 'living in the Midlands, I enjoy short sea trips. I hope

you don't suffer from *mal de mer*, by the way?' He shot
her a sharp glance from under his brow.

'Don't worry. I won't embarrass you,' Merrill
snapped.

'Good. Then there's nothing to worry about.'

Easy for him to say that, Merrill thought, as she
thankfully sat down at her desk after he'd left. She was
filled with the greatest apprehension about the next
couple of days. If only Luke Travis were—oh, fifty
years old, and paunchy and balding and placid like her
previous employer, she would be looking forward to
this trip. But there was no time to dwell on that now;
in true Travis fashion he had left her with a big
workload which she needed to clear today.

The telephone was already ringing when Merrill
arrived at her office the following morning. Luke's
voice, as clear and incisive as if he stood beside her,
said peremptorily, 'I seem to have forgotten my passport. It's at home on the hall table, I think. Damn fool
thing to do. . . You'll find a set of my house keys in
the office safe and——'

'I'll get over there when I've checked the mail,'
Merrill cut in quickly, 'and I'll bring your passport with
me.'

'Good. See you this afternoon, then.' The line went
dead before she could say goodbye.

Four Winds was built on rising ground on the north-
ern outskirts of the city, and Merrill studied it with
interest as she got out of her car. It was, she reflected,
exactly the kind of place a high-flier like Luke would
choose. Distinctive and different. From where she
stood on the gravelled forecourt, she saw that the flight
of steps ahead led up to the living accommodation at
the higher level, no doubt to exploit the panoramic
view, while below, built into the slope, were the

garages and stores. The house had been designed to make the most of natural materials, from the hand-hewn greenish slates of the roof to the cool grey stone walls which set off various shrubs and some of the roses he had spoken of. It must look a picture in the summer! she thought, her gaze lifting to the sweeping roofline which suggested a sense of soaring, almost of weightlessness.

The effect, Merrill noticed a few moments later, had been carried into the interior. There was a spaciousness and simplicity of line that made a perfect foil for the few touches of vibrant colour that drew the eye, and yet the whole effect was completely uncontrived, as if it had all come together naturally. And that, too, was Luke, she thought—the sure touch, the instinctive flair and selection.

For a moment she stood looking around the wide hall, closely carpeted in dark, velvety blue which lent an added drama to the vivid Impressionist paintings, the apricot-coloured Knole settee. But the table, simple, modern, deeply polished, bore only a slim white lamp. No passport.

Merrill hesitated. Time was passing, and she had to catch that London train. Just the prospect of being late was enough to bring her out in a sweat of fear. And she had to find Luke's passport; that was crucial. She opened the first door leading off the hall to find only a cloakroom. Beyond the hall was a lounge with wide views over the trees on the slope below. But there was no time to admire the view, no time for more than a swift impression of airiness and light, of deep, comfort-able furniture in maize-coloured linen, before she closed the door quickly. There was a dining-room, its vast table formed of two carved stone pillars supporting a smoked-glass top, and there was a bedroom with a display of silver-topped toilet jars, and a fragile lacy négligé hanging on the door. Merrill's face burned. Damn the man, she hadn't bargained for a Peeping Tom role! I don't want to know whether or not he shares his life with anyone, she thought fiercely, slamming the door behind her.

Then she was in another bedroom which could only be Luke's, and on the chest by the window lay the passport. She snatched it up and thrust it into her bag, her glance flicking up to yet another magnificent view.

It was only when she had closed the door behind her and was hurrying along the corridor that led back into the hall that she noticed the painting. Arrested by recognition, she stared at the picture—one of Elise's best—of a blind gypsy. The earthy colours, the red scarf, the brown hands lying idle across the strings of a violin, the brown, dreaming face. . . The last time she had seen it was in Elise's studio. Her eyes were blurred by sudden tears as she locked the door behind her.

As she drove away her heart speeded up into an erratic, agitated rhythm. Calm down, she told herself, through gritted teeth. Why the sudden rush of adrenalin? Hadn't she already known the score—Luke's one-time involvement with Elise? And his present involvement with another woman was patently obvious by that exquisite négligé, the array on the dressing-table. But, with a man of Luke's charisma, that was only to be expected. So why the sudden blaze?

But the sight of Elise's work, hanging in Luke's house, had caught her unawares, underlining her loss and, at the same time, reminding her that on the only occasion when Elise's name had been mentioned Luke had adopted an attitude of total indifference, not even bothering to mention that he owned one of Elise's paintings. It was odd, to say the least!

However, long before Merrill reached London she regained her composure, and she handed over Luke's passport without a blink, seeing no necessity to tell him that she'd had to search his house for it.

During the short sea crossing to Zeebrugge Luke occupied himself making notes on his meeting of the previous evening, and thankfully Merrill opened the paperback she had brought with her, her favourite author's latest suspense novel. Yet she couldn't lose herself in the story; the movements of Luke's hand as he made lightning sketches, the lazy, sinuous stretching of his legs as he shifted his position impinged upon her concentration, and she found herself reading the same page over and over.

'Good book?' he asked as the shoreline became visible through a drift of sea fret.

Merrill had the distinct feeling that he had noticed her distraction and she could only hope he hadn't guessed the reason for it.

'Oh, very good,' she said enthusiastically. 'I can't wait to get back to it.'

'Well, don't bank on doing a lot of reading while we're here. It is a business trip, you know.'

She followed him on to the train for the short journey to Bruges. He had put away his notes and now talked so entertainingly about earlier visits to the city and about its importance during the Middle Ages that Merrill found herself disarmed and interested.

'I like it in the winter,' he said finally. 'It has so much atmosphere that one can almost see the medieval wool merchants going about their business. But now, at this time of the year, the daffodils will be in bloom in the Beguinage—you must go and see them.'

Merrill smiled. 'I intend to. I read up a little about the place.'

'Do you research everything so thoroughly?' he asked, watching her quizzically.

'If I can. Is something wrong with that?'

'Not at all. I applaud it.' His eyes swept her figure, neat and businesslike in her shadow-check grey suit with the fuchsia-coloured shirt that exactly matched her short, roomy coat.

Merrill thought he was going to say something more, but the train drew into Bruges, and a little while later she closed the door of her hotel room, thankful to be alone. So far, it had been a rather wearing day, fraught with strange emotions, and it wasn't over yet. She had arranged to meet Luke in the bar for a drink, and she hoped that he had a dinner engagement so that she would be left to her own devices afterwards. She could cope well enough with him in the office where their point of contact was work, but occasional moments—like last Saturday, sitting in the sunshine in the garden of her flat, and today on the train—had shown her a glimpse of Luke the man, not simply Luke the employer. And there was no escaping the fact that he had more than his fair quota of attraction. And it reached her; in a totally unwelcome manner she seemed trapped in a web spun by golden eyes, a harshly boned face, a sensual mouth that often hid its humour. The last thing in the world she needed was to be attracted to the man who had been Elise's lover—even if he weren't already engaged in a live-in relationship with another woman!

Quickly she unpacked, took a brisk shower and dressed carefully in a high-necked dress of watermelon-pink wool, piling up her dark hair at the back so that her neck rose, long and slender, from the draped collar, showing to advantage the chunky silver earrings. A critical glance in the mirror as she thrust her feet into

high-heeled black shoes revealed that she was looking
her best. She needed every scrap of self-confidence she
could rustle up, she thought, then grinned crookedly at
the wary light in her eyes reflected by the glass.

Luke was leaning against the bar as she went down
the stairs. He slewed round, saw her, then straightened. For a second their glances leapt to meet each
other, locking for a heart-stopping moment in a recognition that seemed more than merely superficial.
Merrill's pulse quickened dangerously, but she forced
herself to walk towards him smoothly, her mouth lifting
in a pleasant social smile.

'Should I start by saying all the usual, very appropri-
ate things?' he asked lightly as he took their drinks
over to a small table near the cavernous fireplace.

'Such as?' Merrill took a sip of her martini, eyeing
him over the rim of her glass.

'Oh, you know. . . Don't be coy, Merrill.' But he
was smiling, and it occurred to her that recently he had
smiled quite frequently. And that, too, was disarming.
She stared through the long net curtains out on to the
'tZand, empty now in the thickening twilight, and
suddenly her wariness dissolved. Here she was, in a
strange country, in a beautiful medieval city, with a
man who stood head and shoulders above the others in
the lounge, so why not enjoy it? Why not go along with
Luke's expansive mood for just so long as it took to
finish her drink? What harm could *that* do?

'I'm not being coy,' she said, laughing. 'How do I
know what you consider to be the "usual, very apro-
priate things"?'

'Then I'll tell you: in a nutshell, you look soft and
warm and human. Not to mention lovely and a few
other superlatives.'

'Steady!' she warned, still laughing. 'There's no need

to go overboard. Anyway, I thought this was strictly a business trip,' she added, a glint of mischief in her eyes.

'It is, but even the most hard-pressed executive owes it to himself to relax occasionally and give himself some space.'

'And this is relaxation?' She felt anything but relaxed; stimulated, scintillating—yes. Relaxed? Definitely not.

'For me, yes. And I'd thought to follow it up with a gourmet meal somewhere. It's been quite a day, hasn't it? So drink up, then get your coat. And you'd better change those shoes. They're not designed to cope with cobbled streets.'

'So we're going for a walk, I take it? This is your fresh-air-and-exercise space, then?'

He laughed. 'Bruges is a place to discover on foot, as you'll find out. Any objection? Perhaps you'd rather stay here and read your riveting book. You certainly didn't get very far with it on the boat,' he added slyly.

So he *had* noticed!

She was spared thinking of a suitable comment as he stood up. 'Your coat,' he prompted, 'and then we should go. I took the liberty of reserving a table for us.'

'Then you took rather a lot for granted, didn't you?' Merrill tried unsuccessfully to introduce a note of matter-of-fact severity into her voice, but it didn't work. How difficult it was to try to keep her feet on the ground, when inside she felt as if she were poised on the brink of a wild and wonderful adventure.

'It was a risk,' he agreed silkily, 'but I considered it well worth it. And after all, I knew that you couldn't plead a prior engagement.'

At the foot of the stairs Merrill turned to face him.

Her eyes were shining, and she glowed with an inner warmth. How long it seemed since she'd had a touch of glamour in her life! And if this was nothing more, at least it had all the trappings of a glamorous evening. 'You're incorrigible,' she said.

He moved his broad shoulders in the suggestion of a shrug. 'I prefer to think of myself as merely enterprising,' he remarked carelessly. 'And *you*—well, we'll talk about *you* later.'

Only for a brief moment while Merrill was changing her shoes did she know a fleeting reservation. But she couldn't draw back now; she didn't even want to. Tonight was something special, a one-off occasion, time out.

As they walked over the little grey bridges that spanned the canals, as she stared up at tall Dutch gables or floodlit towers, Luke told her a little of the history of the city. The pressure of his hand under her elbow was intimate and compelling, and Merrill was filled with a sense of sharing the night and the splendour with the one man right for the occasion.

'I hope you're hungry,' Luke remarked, as they faced each other across a beautifully appointed table in a restaurant overlooking the canal. 'This is going to be a meal to remember.'

'I've found the whole evening so far unforgettable,' Merrill said softly, adding hurriedly, 'It's such a beautiful place, so atmospheric, and——' She shrugged, laughing a little. 'My turn now for the superlatives.'

'Well, perhaps it's simply—one of those nights,' Luke said thoughtfully. 'They happen rarely, but when they do then everything is absolutely perfect. Which brings me to your dress. Top marks; it's the perfect colour for you.'

He put his elbows on the table, interlacing his fingers

and resting his chin on them, gazing at her seriously, and Merrill fought against the glow his words had lit inside her. It was *too* perfect—all of it! Suddenly the memory of the négligé hanging on the door in Luke's house and Elise's painting in the corridor outside his room struck a chill. She sought refuge in small talk, but during the meal, in spite of herself, her blood began its crazy dance again as Luke's golden gaze weakened her.

Afterwards, when coffee was served together with delectable hand-made chocolates, Merrill tried again to bring herself down to earth. 'You mentioned that you had a half-brother,' she murmured, 'and that he'd be coming into Woodline Design.'

'Rob? Yes, that's right. He's much younger than me, of course.'

'Does he live with you?' Mentally Merrill drew a quick plan of Four Winds. She couldn't remember seeing a room which might be Rob's, but of course she hadn't had to explore the entire house before finding the passport.

Luke laughed. 'No, thank heaven. I live alone for most of the time—apart from Stella, that is. But she's not there often.'

Stella, the owner of the négligé. Merrill's heart plumetted as the wheel turned full circle again. Everything came back. . . Elise. Now Stella. She looked at the man sitting opposite her, and was suffused with a sense of loss. What on earth was she doing allowing herself to become involved in the fairy-tale of this enchantment?

'Yes,' Luke went on, his eyes half closed as he gently swilled his brandy round his glass, 'Stella's my step-mother. My own mother is dead, and my father married again—a much younger woman. Rob is the offspring of that union. So Stella lives with me—in the proper conventional manner of course. She's off on a cruise at the moment.'

Merrill took a sip of her cognac to hide the spontaneity of her relief and stared out of the window to the floodlit weeping willow on the opposite bank drooping its spring-green hair towards the water.

'You suddenly seem very happy, very much at peace with the world,' Luke smiled, watching her.

But he had used the wrong word; 'peace' was far from the correct description of Merrill's emotions, but. . . 'Well, who wouldn't be happy?' she said softly. 'I had no idea that business trips could be like this.'

'Nor had I.' He laughed and summoned the bill. 'But tomorrow you'll see the other side of the coin. I should warn you, it'll be hectic, and we'll be making an early start.'

'I'll be ready,' she said stoutly.

He laughed again. 'That's my girl.'

Three casual little words shouldn't assume such importance, Merrill thought, dazed, as they walked back through the darkness.

At the hotel Luke collected both keys from the night porter, and when they reached her room he unlocked the door and held it open for her, then closed it behind him.

They stood facing each other for a moment in silence. Luke's eyes glinted, smiling, enticing. . . Then his hands dropped lightly on Merrill's shoulders, moving sensuously and disturbing the folds of pink wool until his palms lay against the skin of her nape. She closed her eyes for a moment, fighting the tremor that began somewhere in the pit of her stomach. She knew what was coming; she wanted it to happen. All her senses cried out for him. Yet she was gripped by a paralysis born of her long-standing mistrust of him. This, after all, was the man who had made love to Elise, made an impact strong enough to perhaps contribute to Elise's death. And yet he could dismiss that affair—and Elise—as if they had meant nothing. As no doubt he would dismiss this evening—part of a planned relaxation programme during a hectic business trip. After all, hadn't these past weeks taught Merrill that business was the only thing that really mattered to him?

And yet still she stood there, transfixed by the demands in his eyes, powerless to move.

His lips, when they touched hers, were warm, tasting very slightly and pleasantly of cognac. His kiss was leisurely as if they had all the time in the world to explore each other, and he could afford to wait for her response, confident in his own powers of arousing it.

Merrill kept her lips tightly closed, set hard against the turbulent need that whirled inside her, and after a little while Luke drew back. His eyes had darkened with desire, but there was bafflement there, too.

'Do you usually kiss like that?' he said, very softly.

'I wasn't kissing,' Merrill whispered.

'My point exactly. Any particular reason? Or shouldn't I ask?'

Despite his soft tone his words held a chip of flint, and Merrill found herself able to move away and rearrange the folds of her neckline with miraculously steady fingers. 'Do you believe in fairy-tales?' she asked. 'And, specifically, what do you think of the Cinderella story?'

His brows drew together in a sudden spasm of irritation.

'What are you talking about?'

'Oh, *you* know. . . After the ball Cinderella returns to her kitchen and her ashes——'

'And you're Cinderella, and the ball is over? Is that what you're saying?'

'Something like that.' Merrill forced a bright smile. 'I'm simply your assistant, Luke. We're here for business reasons; otherwise we *wouldn't* be here. And, by your own admission, we've got a heavy day tomorrow.'

From one of the city's belfries midnight chimed.

'I see,' Luke said tightly. 'Well, like so much else tonight, your timing's perfect.'

'Purely coincidental,' Merrill murmured. She wished that he would go. She longed to be back in his arms, to let his lips open her own, to melt against him, to give—and to take—the delight which instinctively she knew they could create together. He was the right man. Yet on all other scores he was the *wrong* man. Absolutely!

'Well,' he said, laconic now, and distant, 'it was a great ball while it lasted.'

'*Exactly*.' Merrill threw him a friendly smile and removed one earring. 'And thank you so much. . . What time shall I see you in the morning?'

'Make it eight-thirty, and be ready to go.'

When he had left Merrill breathed a sigh of relief, but as she sat at the dressing-table removing her make-up something inside her wept. It's no good, she rebuked herself sternly; there's no future in feeling like this about Luke Travis. You took the job with him simply to clear up a mystery. You're no nearer solving it yet, and you simply can't afford to complicate the issue by falling in love with him. He's your boss, nothing more. And that's how it must stay.

She lay sleepless for so long—trying to get a grip on the situation, convincing herself that one kiss, one evening that held all the trimmings of romance had no real value—that she awoke late. Eight-thirty, he'd said, and it was already a few minutes past that! No doubt he was waiting for her in the foyer, champing at her non-appearance.

When she went down she was surprised to see that Luke was still in the dining-room, finishing his breakfast. He frowned as she approached. 'I was just about to leave,' he said brusquely. 'I won't be needing you this morning after all.'

'Oh?' Was this his way of cutting her down to size? Merrill wondered. A reprisal for her unwillingness to co-operate last night? She sat down and poured a glass of orange juice.

'I've had a message from one of the members of the consortium that he's providing a multi-lingual stenographer. He telephoned me first thing.'

Merrill nodded. 'I see.'

'Did you sleep well?' he asked politely.

'Never better,' Merrill answered, helping herself to rolls and butter. It looked as if Luke's pride had allowed him to draw a veil over last night's final moments, and she was grateful for it. 'And you?'

'Oh, fine,' he said easily, standing up. 'I'll be off, then.'

Merrill stared at the crumbly mess she was making on her plate. What was it about a waistcoat that was so piercingly sexy? she wondered dully. Not that Luke needed any sartorial props; he was just naturally sensuously exciting as she had always suspected, and now knew to her cost. And he couldn't have reached his present age—thirty-six, wasn't it?—without becoming fully aware of it; and no doubt that had prompted last night's little episode.

She realised that he was still speaking, and she answered vaguely, 'Do? Oh, don't worry about me. I'll see some of the sights, search out that Michaelangelo you spoke of. I'm perfectly capable of looking after myself.'

He smiled, but his narrowed eyes were hard. 'I don't doubt it for a moment.'

Merrill turned uninterestedly away and lifted the coffee-pot as the dining-room door swung violently shut behind him.

CHAPTER FOUR

THIS was such a beautiful city, Merrill thought a couple of hours later as she paid for her coffee and left the pavement café. The Markt was bathed in spring sunshine, and everywhere looked so clean and pristine as befitted the fine morning. She had succeeded in putting Luke out of her thoughts by concentrating purely on each present moment, each new impression, with the same degree of single-mindedness that he himself was capable of, and with a sense of pleasant anticipation she studied her map and set out to see some of the art treasures.

In the little garden of the Hof Arents she stopped to admire the modern sculptures of the Four Horsemen of the Apocalypse when a voice behind her said, 'Merrill—Merrill Stanton. . .! I thought I caught a glimpse of you in the Brangwyn Museum, but——'

Merrill spun round quickly, her eyebrows arched in surprise. 'It's——' She tried to place the faint West Country burr in his voice. 'It's Richard. . .' Her voice faded.

'Come on,' he laughed. 'Admit it; you've forgotten.' Blue eyes twinkled at her. 'Or perhaps you never knew it. The name's Richard Stirling. And let me jog your memory further. We met at Elise's cottage about eighteen months ago, remember? A barbecue, a crowded lawn, spilt beer on the kitchen floor, and——'

'And I was mopping up,' Merrill supplied. 'Yes, I do remember. You called me Cinderella.'

Momentarily, recalling her conversation with Luke

last night, her smile wavered. What a coincidence that this particular name should crop up twice within twenty-four hours!

'Did I? Well, I shouldn't have done.' Richard was still smiling, a pleasant, crooked smile in a plain, nice, comfortable face. 'Merrill is far lovelier.' He paused, then said gently, 'I heard about Elise. I'm sorry. . . A brilliant career—just wiped out.'

'Yes.' Merrill nodded. There was nothing she could add.

Then Richard went on conversationally, 'And what are you doing in Bruges?'

'I'm on a business trip with my boss.' Merrill was glad to change the subject. 'However, he's tied up this morning, so I'm taking a look around.' After the hours spent in Luke's disturbing company it came as a relief to hold a light, uncomplicated conversation with an ordinary guy. 'And how about you? A holiday?'

'No such luck. Research. I'm contributing to a book on art, and as Brangwyn worked with William Morris for a time, and some of his work is exhibited here, I thought I'd take a look-see for myself. I always find art galleries and museums hungry work, though. I don't suppose you're free for lunch? Or do you have to report back to the boss?'

Merrill laughed. 'I'm not sure what time he'll be through with his meeting, but perhaps I'd better get back to the hotel and show willing just in case he's there.'

'Hmm, pity.' Richard squinted up at the sun then fell into step beside her. 'Well, what about dinner tonight? I expect you're free in the evenings?'

'Ye-es, I think so; in fact I'm sure I am.' There was no chance that Luke would court a second rebuff, she thought. She had left him in no doubt about her reaction to his overtures. But even now the remembrance of his arms around her sent a hungry little sensor probing through her.

'Good.' Richard's voice cut into her thoughts as he took her arm to draw her back from a horse-drawn carriage laden with tourists on a sightseeing trip. 'Well, give me the name of your hotel, then, and I'll call for you at, say, seven. And if by any chance you can't manage dinner tonight perhaps we can at least have a drink together and fix some other time.'

'I'll look forward to it,' Merrill smiled.

Richard's hand gripped hers firmly for moment, then he was striding away, his loose coat flapping, his rather long hair ruffled by the wind that stirred the daffodils on the grass around them.

Merrill looked at her watch. After one! The morning had flown, and if Luke was back he wouldn't be too pleased to find her still missing. However, as she passed the reception desk she noticed that his key was still on its hook. She ordered sandwiches and coffee and settled down in the lounge to wait for him.

She was staring out of the window across the open space of the 'tZand when he came in. Instantly the air of the quiet lounge seemed to stir, to gather vibrations as if his arrival ushered in a powerful force. Merrill's inner sensors caught the onslaught, and her heart lurched, tipping her back into the treacherous quicksands of desire and suspicion.

His grey whipcord coat with its black velvet collar hung open, and he came quickly across with that purposeful step which was one of the first things she had noticed about him. Why couldn't he be less— positive? she wondered dully. And why did the impact of his presence provoke such an undeniable response

in her when, earlier, she had felt that she had everything under control?

She watched him warily as he dropped his briefcase
on to the chair next to her own and perched on the
arm, stretching out long legs, and running his fingers
through his hair. 'Well?' he said. 'Had a good
morning?'

'Lovely,' she answered stiltedly. 'And you? How did
the meeting go?' Strictly business, her inner resolve
prompted. Don't get into any conversations about
sitting in the sunshine drinking coffee, or the unforgettable paintings in the Memling Museum, or the daffodils dancing in the gardens at the Beguinage. 'The
contract? Were you able to——?'

Luke smiled broadly. 'A most successful morning.
My seating unit design for the conference centre has
been approved. We'll need to sub-contract, of course,
but I'll be at the helm.'

Merrill sent him a quizzical glance. Wasn't he always
at the helm?

'And I don't need to tell you,' he continued, 'that
this means a lot to Woodline. Full order books, not to
mention the prestige. . . And, I might add, the clarity
of your notes was greatly appreciated.'

His enthusiasm was infectious, and as Merrill looked
up at the lively amber glint in his eyes she couldn't
suppress a smile. 'Glad to be of use,' she murmured
meekly.

He looked at her for a long, silent moment, and
Merrill dragged her gaze away with difficulty, maddened by her erratic heartbeat. Damn it, she wailed
silently, if he could do this to her with a mere glance,
what might he have achieved last night if she hadn't
found the strength to conclude that little episode when
she did?

He stood up abruptly. 'I'm going to order some soup or something, then we'll get our heads together in the corner. There are a few finer details to be worked out, a couple of modifications and so on, and some more costing. I'll need to make a telephone call to Mike. . . So go get your notebook and the calculator, will you? I'll meet you in half an hour.'

It was after six o'clock when they finished. Merrill's head swam, but Luke leaned back with a grunt of satisfaction. 'What would I do without you?' he said. 'And we've both earned a drink. Sit there. I'll bring them.'

'You're like a tornado,' Merrill said, when he came back. 'Or perhaps I mean a hurricane. Well, whatever—you drive everything before you. Nothing gets in your way—or, if it does, you simply demolish it.'

He pulled down his mouth as he studied his glass. 'Ah,' he said softly, 'if only that were true! I'm as fallible as the next man. Or hadn't you noticed? No, probably not. Still,' he conceded reflectively, 'there might be something in what you say. Certainly I don't let small things stand in my way when I really set out to achieve my ends.'

'There's a word for that,' Merrill countered. 'Ruthless.'

'And that's what you think of me?'

For a moment Merrill wondered if her description had hurt him, but his expression was sufficiently aloof to bounce off any information he did not wish to hear. And she had no intention of telling him just what she *did* think of him, not that it would have made sense, anyway—either to him or, more importantly, to herself.

She drained her glass quickly and stood up. 'Thank

you for the drink. If you'll excuse me I'll go up and shower and change.'

Politely he got up, handing her the notebook and her handbag. 'I'd thought we might safely have dinner here tonight. The streets of a city as atmospheric and romantic as Bruges do strange things to a man. If not to a woman,' he added, apparently as an afterthought.

Merrill felt her face grow warm at this indirect reference to her rebuff of the previous evening. She paused uncertainly. 'Is it a working dinner?' she asked. 'I mean, should I——'

'No, you won't be needing your notebook,' he said with a grin. 'Don't you think we've done enough today?'

She bit her lip, nodding.

'Do I detect a note of reluctance?' he said wryly. 'Don't worry. When the meal is over you'll be perfectly free to return to that absorbing book of yours.' When she didn't immediately react, he went on drily, 'I assume you *are* intending to eat tonight? Then what's more natural than for two business colleagues staying in the same hotel to dine together?'

'I'm sorry,' Merrill said, blindly thrusting her notebook into her handbag, 'but I already have a date.'

There was an instant's hush. 'Have you, now?' he said softly. 'Well, well. It didn't take you long, did it? I'd forgotten your talent for sociability.'

'What do you mean?' Merrill snapped.

His face was infuriatingly bland as he answered, 'Didn't you tell me that night when I gave you a lift home that your life fairly buzzed with—shall we say—events?'

Merrill looked down; it was true. She had deliberately given him that impression simply because she hadn't wanted to look lonely and pathetic in his eyes.

'But,' he went on inexorably, 'I hadn't expected you to achieve the desired result in one short morning in a strange city. You certainly don't let the grass grow, do you?'

'That's quite uncalled for,' she retorted. 'And if the business of the day is concluded——'

'How prissy you can sound at times, Merrill,' he drawled.

'The point I was trying to make,' she persisted hotly, 'was that my off-duty time is surely my own.'

He moved his hand in a negligent gesture. 'Oh, quite so. I wouldn't dream of infringing on your liberty. It must have been a very interesting morning indeed.'

'It was,' Merrill flashed. 'Fantastic. But for your information——'

Luke lifted a silencing, imperious hand. 'Spare me the details,' he murmured silkily. 'You made it abundantly clear that you have one hell of a good social life at home. Stupid of me not to realise that here, also. . . Still, far be it from me to stand in the way of close international relations. . .'

'You know, I don't have to take this from you,' Merrill breathed.

'Quite right. You don't have to do anything, apart from provide me with the back-up I need in business.'

For a moment she stared up at him, her fists clenched at her sides, her grey eyes filled with a crystalline chill totally at variance with the molten rage that consumed her. 'You needn't remind me of that fact,' she said cuttingly. 'I keep it firmly before me *all* the time.' And that, she hoped, was a sufficiently pointed allusion to last night's abortive episode.

'Oh, yes, I had noticed.' He flicked a speck from his lapel with a careless gesture, then he turned to pick up his briefcase. 'So I'll say goodnight. Have fun. But there, I don't have to tell you that, do I? However, don't overdo it. We're off to Ghent tomorrow, and it's going to be a long, long day.'

He turned on his heel and left the room. Merrill put her hands against her hot cheeks for a moment. He was impossible! Although she had rejected his dinner invitation, somehow he had come out of the scene the victor. Obviously he assumed that she had picked up some instant Romeo, and it was clear from his tone and expression that he condemned her as cheap and shallow.

He can think what he likes, she stormed silently, under the tingling needles of water in the shower. A few hours in Richard's company was just the antidote she needed to Luke's volatility.

During the evening, however, Merrill developed a raging headache and had to force an interest in Richard's conversation. It was just as well, she thought ruefully, that he was an easy, undemanding companion, and had it not been for the throbbing behind her eyes she might have considered the evening pleasant enough. He had known Elise only slightly and seemed to sense that Merrill didn't want to talk about her cousin, and he confined his conversation to holidays, recent travel and his work.

When they finally said goodnight outside the hotel it was with a vague arrangement to meet again some time. 'I'll be travelling around a bit, I expect,' he said, smiling, 'so when I'm in your part of the world I'll look you up. And thanks, Merrill, for taking pity on a lonely traveller.'

He dropped a light kiss on her cheek and strode off across the empty square.

Merrill went straight up to her room, relieved to be

alone and quiet at last, and as she undressed for bed she thought that she heard the door to Luke's room open and close again. She wondered idly how he had occupied the evening, then felt her face burn at the memory of his low opinion of her. It was the wrong kind of thought to ponder when all she wanted was to sleep away her headache and awake refreshed and ready for whatever challenge the next day would offer.

There were two meetings to attend in Ghent, the second one lasting into the evening, and Merrill's notebook filled rapidly, predicting several busy days when she got back. She was looking forward to getting home again, back to her flat and out of Luke's orbit after office hours.

Eventually the meeting closed and Merrill put her notebook away and waited quietly by the door as Luke made his farewells to the others. She hoped he wouldn't come up with any suggestions about spending the evening together. But no, on second thoughts, she decided he was unlikely to lay himself open to further rejection. So—a long, hot bath, dinner in her room with her book, then an early night. And home tomorrow! She felt an inward sense of release.

Then Luke was beside her. 'We've been invited out to dinner this evening,' he said tersely. 'In the circumstances I could hardly refuse.'

'Fine,' Merrill said blithely. 'You keep the hired car, and I'll take the train back to Bruges. It's a good rail service. I took the precaution of looking it up in case——'

'Efficient as always,' he said drily, 'but you've missed the point. I said *we've* been invited. Look,' he hurried on as Merrill turned away to hide her dismayed expression, 'Sam Holdsworth's an important contact. He and his wife have a place here in Ghent, and he's asked us both over. I've accepted,' he added baldly, after a moment.

'Then you had no right to speak for me,' Merrill whispered in hushed irritation, 'no right to take it for granted that——'

Luke's expression contained an equal irritation. 'I do apologise if I've upset your social plans for this evening,' he said with heavy sarcasm, 'but this is important to me, and it's all in the line of business. And,' he added with a malevolent glint in his eyes, 'at your interview I did point out that I wasn't offering a nine-to-five sinecure.'

Merrill sighed. 'Oh, all right,' she muttered after a moment. 'Put like that, I suppose I've no choice.'

'No,' Luke said calmly, 'you haven't really. So do you think that we could put our differences aside for just one evening? Ah, here comes Sam now. . . And one other thing—could you possibly manage to look a little less disgruntled?'

Merrill was saved a reply as they were both enveloped in Sam's breezy *bonhomie*. He took an arm of each of them and hurried them out of the building and down the steps. 'Follow my car,' he grinned. 'Home's only ten minutes' drive.'

Luke was silent until he drew up outside an imposingly formal grey stone house, then as he switched off the ignition he said, in tones of mock-comfort, 'Brace up, Merrill. Of course, I can't pretend that this evening can compete with the delights of your date last night, but as it's our last evening here you should make the most of it—*without* the continental touch.'

Merrill flicked him a scornful glance. Apparently he was under the impression that she had arranged to see Richard again tonight; he was also under the delusion that Richard was a Belgian whom she had just happened to pick up. But why bother to enlighten him? He would only assume that she attached some importance to his opinion and take it as a compliment. And why should it matter what he thought? Once this trip was over she would let him know her real reason for taking this job with Woodline Design, then she would say goodbye. How chagrined he would be to learn that she hadn't sought the interview in the first place; that had been just another of the wrong conclusions that he had drawn about her! She savoured the prospect with a tiny smile—half rueful, half triumphant—which widened into greeting as Sam introduced his wife, Anna, and Merrill put her private plans firmly into the background.

Upstairs in the bathroom where Anna had taken Merrill to freshen up, she caught a glimpse of her reflection in the mirror. 'It's been a long day,' she grinned, 'and it shows!'

'Luke been giving you a hard time?' Anna smiled. 'He's a ball of fire, I know. Look, why not have a quick bath? Dinner won't be ready for another hour or so.' Even as she spoke she was taking a fleecy rose-coloured towel out of the linen press, turning on the water, unscrewing a flask of bath essence which perfumed the rising steam. She smiled again. 'You can hardly refuse now. I'll leave you to it, then.'

A ten-minute soak worked wonders on Merrill's jaded sense of well-being, and when she went down she found the three of them seated around a huge log fire. It soon became clear that Sam and Luke had many acquaintances in common; they chatted easily, and Anna was skilful at drawing Merrill into the conversation. By the time they sat down to a light but elegant dinner, a warm rapport had grown between the two women.

Luke showed yet another side of his personality: he laughed a lot, amusing them with a fund of stories, some of which, Merrill conceded with grudging admiration, were told against himself. Almost against her will she found herself glad to be there.

'What a gorgeous man to work for,' Anna confided, as she and Merrill stacked the dishwasher later. 'Dynamic and demanding, I guess——'

'You could say that,' Merrill agreed vaguely. She was beginning to regret that Sam had insisted on keeping her wine glass filled during the meal. She felt delightfully relaxed and slightly unreal, and her mouth seemed incapable of shaping anything but a broad smile.

'So you live near Sherwood Forest,' Anna remarked. 'I don't know that part of England. Is it as I imagine— masses of oak trees and birds and secret glades haunted by the ghosts of Robin Hood and his Merrie Men?'

'Not forgetting Maid Marian,' Merrill laughed. 'Well, there are certainly lots of trees, including one known as the Major Oak which gives strength to the legend. . . And it can seem quite ghostly and atmospheric on a misty November afternoon, but I've never seen any ghosts there. I've got a cottage in one of the Forest villages, but it's tenanted at the moment, and I live in town.' She straightened up. 'Look, Anna, the next time you come to England let me know. If you enjoy walking you'll love the Forest. Once away from the car parks you could be the only person in the world.'

'That's great. We'll fix it.' Anna linked her arm with Merrill's as they went to rejoin the men. 'What a pity that you're going back tomorrow. We could have come over to Bruges in the evening and dined together at the Duc de Bourgogne.'

Merrill went over to the wide settee and sank down into the feather cushions. Her limbs felt disconcertingly light, and she was having the greatest difficulty wiping the smile from her face as Luke placed a cushion behind her shoulders. After a moment she realised that he was extolling her virtues as a personal assistant.

'You must let me know your secret,' Sam laughed, when Luke finished, halted by the embarrassed blush which was spreading over Merrill's face. 'I have a big turnover in secretaries, if I may put it that way. Most inconvenient at times. Perhaps,' he went on, turning to Merrill, 'you've got a friend who'd like a job in Ghent?'

Merrill made a determined effort to pull herself out of the glow induced by the wine and Luke's compliments. 'No such luck, Sam. I'm sorry.'

'I think I probably owe a lot to Merrill's previous employer,' Luke smiled. 'She held down quite a high-powered job in London before she came to me.'

'Well, I didn't actually,' Merrill heard herself admitting honestly. 'My boss was a hypochondriac, and the most important item of furniture in the office was the cabinet where he kept his pills and potions. Every three months or so I'd clear it of all the wonder remedies he'd accumulated, but within a week he'd have discovered some other miracle medicine. He was a darling, though,' she added, absently taking a sip of the brandy which had somehow appeared on the table beside her. 'Now if the first symptom of illness came anywhere near Luke——' She turned to him, her eyes mischievous between the sweep of dark lashes, 'If——'

'Yes?' Luke purred. 'You were saying?'

'Simply that you would damn it as a diabolical liberty and banish it,' Merrill finished quickly, sharply aware of a sudden spark which, for no apparent reason, flared between them.

'Oh, dear,' Luke grinned. 'I hadn't realised that I needed to be a hypochondriac to qualify for your— affections.'

The others laughed, but Merrill sensed the derision behind his words—a derision born of his opinion of her.

'And,' he pursued pleasantly, 'I certainly hadn't guessed that you had actually gone to the trouble of speculating on my reactions—to illness or to anything else,' he added quietly.

Somehow he seemed to have cornered Merrill into a trap. She realised that his tone owed its pleasantness to the presence of Sam and Anna. Had she been alone with Luke, no doubt his words would have been spiked with malice.

Discomfited, she managed a light laugh. 'But of course I speculate!' she exclaimed. 'A good assistant studies her boss, almost to the extent of developing psychic powers to indicate what he wants almost before he himself knows.'

'Is that right?' Sam asked. 'Then obviously I've been looking for the wrong qualities in my secretaries.'

'I think I know what quality you were seeing when you engaged the last one,' Anna teased affectionately. 'And obviously she had the wrong idea about what was expected of her!'

'Oh, well,' Sam said easily, 'can I help it if I ooze charm from every pore?'

Luke and Merrill joined in the laughter, then Luke put down his glass and stood up. 'We really must be on our way,' he murmured. 'We're leaving early tomorrow.' He stretched out a hand to Merrill, and she found that she needed it to escape the embrace of the thick, downy cushions. 'I can't thank you both enough for your kindness. I should like to return it, if I may.

Sam, you often come over to England, so why not bring Anna next time, and come up to the Midlands?'

'Yes, let's,' Anna said enthusiastically. 'Merrill's going to show me Sherwood Forest.'

'Well, part of it, at least,' Merrill qualified. Her body seemed too languorous to react quickly to the commands her brain was issuing. She groped vaguely for her handbag, then found that Luke was putting it into her hand. He was grinning devilishly.

'There,' he said soothingly, as they drove away, 'that wasn't too much of an ordeal, was it? Sorry to have messed up your date, but thanks for coming. It helps a lot when the numbers are even.'

'Oh, I enjoyed it,' Merrill said warmly, seeing no need to tell Luke that her evening was free anyway. She waved an airy hand and stifled a yawn. 'They're lovely people. I just wish that Sam hadn't been so generous with the wine, though. I'll probably feel like death tomorrow.' She gazed out over the flat, dark countryside as the lights of Ghent were left behind. A few stars pricked the sky, and in the warmth of the car it seemed that she and Luke were the only two people in the world, travelling through a hushed darkness together. And her eyelids felt so heavy, heavy. . .

As before, she was meltingly aware of the romance of two people, side by side, shoulder almost touching shoulder, breathing the same air, sharing the same journey towards the inevitable dawn. The starlight became entangled in her lashes as her eyes closed. . .

The romantic feeling deepened with his dream-touch; his lips were gentle, warm, coaxing, drawing her into a world of sensual sweetness where intentions and thoughts had no place.

There was only bliss and the joy of revelling in it. Merrill dreamed on in a beautiful drowning. Even her hands were touching something pleasant—silky, soft; she moved her fingers luxuriously, then slowly consciousness returned. Her arms were around his neck, and her hands lay on the velvet collar of his coat. Her mouth was under his, her lips parting beneath the flickering ecstasy of his tongue.

She gasped and pulled away from him. Immediately his hands dropped from her shoulders. He had parked outside the hotel, and in the patchwork of light and shade she saw his half-smile.

'I think that this evening has done you a world of good,' he said softly. 'You're relaxed. It makes a change.'

'Oh?' she said, trying to recover her composure. 'And what has the evening done for *you*?'

'More than you'll ever know, probably,' he answered enigmatically. 'I must admit, though, that I've never had a lady go to sleep on me before.'

Merrill sat up abruptly. 'I'm sorry,' she said tautly. 'I don't usually do that, but it has been a long day.'

'You look quite different when you're asleep,' he mused. 'The tension is gone—that watchful, catlike wariness that you usually project. Instead, you——'

Merrill tore her gaze away from the hard planes of his face, polished by the lamplight, the mysterious, exciting shadows around his eyes. She snapped open her handbag blindly with a sense of gathering panic. Inside the confines of the car the atmosphere pulsed to the same demented rhythm that thrummed in her veins. 'I think—I've lost my—pen,' she whispered inanely.

'Damn your pen! Look, the other night when I. . .' His words faded, and he put his hands on her shoulders again and turned her face him, holding her gaze by the sheer power of his will until, steeled and strengthened

by her desperate need to break the spell, Merrill
wrenched herself away to open the car door.

'Let's not speak of the other night, shall we?' she
said coolly.

'Why not? Am I supposed to be ashamed of an
ordinary male impulse? Heaven knows, you must have
aroused plenty of men in your time.' He gave a harsh
laugh.

Merrill's colour heightened. 'I haven't logged them
all,' she retorted, 'but now that you come to mention
it——'

'And after you've sent out signals,' he interrupted,
'do you always turn off the transmitter? Or is it just
with me? Am I special?'

'Oh, yes,' Merrill breathed, furious at this reminder
of his low opinion of her morals, 'you're special, all
right. You're an opportunist; I learned that a moment
ago. And you're my boss. But that doesn't give you
any privileges with my private life.'

'Not even one? One tiny privilege,' he sneered,
'when obviously you're not—how can I phrase it
discreetly?—exclusive?'

Merrill tried to swallow her anger. All the earlier
euphoria was dissolved by the vitriolic animosity which
surged between them. Situation normal, she thought
bitterly. How satisfying it would have been to vent her
feelings in one sharp slap of that carved-ivory face!
'Haven't you overlooked something?' she whispered
angrily. 'If—as you seem to think—I'm not—exclusive, then doesn't it also figure that experience might
have taught me discernment, selectivity? I'm sorry if
your pride was hurt that other evening. Should I have
fancied you? And does it always happen to order—for
you?'

'Well, as you said yesterday afternoon,' he retorted, 'I'm ruthless.'

She nodded. 'I'll second that. You'll even stoop to trying to seduce a girl while she's asleep. I really——'

'You'd better get inside,' he bit out suddenly, his eyes glittering under knotted brows. 'I think this conversation's gone far enough.' A moment later she felt his finger and thumb at either side of her elbow pinching like a vice as if he needed to punish her physically. But she bore the pain stoically, trying to comfort herself with the thought that Luke was unaccustomed to failure with women. Well, let him get used to the idea! In some strange way it helped to even the score over Elise.

But where, a small, lost voice mourned inside, was that wonderful feeling now? That sense of utter perfection, that conviction that, for once, she was fully alive? But, of course, that had been simply part of a dream and must be dismissed. Now she was back to reality.

CHAPTER FIVE

As THE taxi pulled away from their hotel the following morning, Luke said, 'I think last night's little exchange of views is best forgotten, don't you?'

Merrill flicked him a sideways glance. He was so—so *together*. Smooth-haired, bright-eyed, immaculate, with the merest hint of a woody, masculine fragrance about him, he looked as if nothing could faze him. By comparison, she felt drained and despondent. However, she gave him a bright smile and murmured, 'Last night's. . .? I don't really remember much about it. As I might have mentioned, Sam was too liberal with the wine.'

Luke nodded, apparently satisfied, and on the journey home he spent much of his time behind a newspaper.

Thank heaven it was all over, Merrill thought, dumping down her suitcase in her flat. Business trip it might have been, but one way and another she seemed to have run the gamut of a vast spectrum of emotions, and now the barriers were up again, firmly in place.

She was niggled by a lingering doubt that she might have played her cards badly. Hypocritical though it was, wouldn't she have been wiser to have led Luke on a little, been a bit more responsive when the opportunity arose? Maybe that way she could have coaxed out a little information about his affair with Elise. But her conscience balked at the idea. For one thing, she wasn't cold-blooded enough to have capitalised on those moments. And for another. . . She shivered, knowing instinctively what would have resulted if she had encouraged Luke the slightest bit. And that, of course, she decided ruefully over a cup of coffee at the kitchen breakfast-bar, would have played right into his hands, seeming to justify his opinion of her. So far as he was concerned, she was fair game; that accounted for his behaviour in her bedroom, the scene in the hired car last night.

Bruges had certainly provided an opportunity for getting to know Luke better, and now Merrill could understand why Elise had fallen in love with him. And if he had meted out to Elise the same unpredictable treatment, the same highs and lows, then it wasn't beyond the bounds of possibility that he was the kind of man who made a girl, driven beyond all logic, all reason, decide that life without him was no longer worth living.

'I loathe and detest you, Luke Travis,' Merrill whispered later, as she hung up the pink dress. 'You might be a whizz at your job, you might have the charisma of ten men, but when it comes down to normal decent human values you're nothing. *Nothing*.'

She blinked away sudden scalding tears, and wearily finished unpacking. But amazingly her dreams were untainted by the intensity of her loathing. Instead was a happy medley of Luke laughing, of taking her hand as they ran up a long flight of grey stone steps towards some vague but wonderful journey's end. And when Merrill awoke the following morning her lips were slightly parted to receive his dream-kiss.

By Monday morning Merrill had succeeded in thrusting the memory of that dream firmly out of her mind. She was oddly reluctant to start the day's work although previously the demands and challenges of working for

Luke had given a spice to her days. And as she pushed open the forest-green doors of Woodline Design she realised with surprise that she hadn't given a thought to Max for some considerable time.

The door connecting her office with Luke's was closed, and Merrill grimaced. If he wanted to remain incommunicado that was fine by her. At least it would give her the opportunity to make a start on her copious notes.

She uncovered her typewriter, flipped open her notebook and was soon immersed in a draft of the lengthy Ghent report. When the buzzer on the wall sounded she jumped, striking a wrong key. Luke had never before found it necessary to summon her by the buzzer, preferring instead to call her name, and so establishing a kind of business-hours informality. But now it looked as if her job might have taken a different turn. Still, if he wanted to formally emphasise the gulf between them, it was all to the good. The few moments of past closeness which they had shared had always left her emotionally upside-down and, inevitably, angry.

As usual he was immaculate in a dark suit with a faint pinstripe, and there was that fastidiousness about him which, somehow, missed being clinical; it emphasised his aloofness, yet it also invited, suggested, lured. . . Merrill's heart lurched miserably. It was utterly beyond comprehension that, mistrusting him as she did, she could never quite succeed in damping down a tiny *frisson* of physical response. It had become part of each morning's routine, almost as if a night's absence—or a weekend's—simply served to burnish his attractions.

She murmured good morning, sat down and stared at her open notebook, the tip of her pen poised above the clean page.

'You didn't tell me that your cousin was dead,' Luke said without preamble, his voice very quiet.

Merrill's head jerked up, and she dropped her notebook, a rush of blood surging into her face. His blunt observation had pulled the ground from beneath her feet. 'Didn't I?' she mumbled, bending, her fingers scrabbling blindly over the fluttering pages.

His topaz gaze was chilling. 'No, you didn't. Any particular reason for the mystery?'

Oh, yes! she wanted to shout. I was waiting for the right moment to find out just how deeply your were involved with Elise. And then I would have made my own judgement about her death. But somehow that right moment never came.

He was watching her closely, a guarded gleam in his eyes, and their wariness served to confirm Merrill's suspicions. 'Perhaps,' he said curtly, 'I ought to rephrase the question. Did you have any particular reason for not mentioning Elise's death?'

Merrill took a deep breath. This was it. Give him enough rope and he would hang himself. 'Maybe I'm not very bright this morning,' she prevaricated, 'but you seem to be implying something. And why *now*? I mean, why have you suddenly brought up the subject of Elise?'

Luke pushed back his chair impatiently and went to stand at the window, looking down, his back towards her.

It's so that I can't see his face, Merrill thought. He's guessed that I suspect something, but he can't possibly know just what, nor how. So he's got to be careful, and he's worried that he might give himself away by some tiny flicker of expression.

'I've raised the subject *now*,' he replied coolly, 'because Mike went over to see her. Or perhaps I should say that Mike went to Bracken Cottage while you and I were in Bruges. She wasn't there, of course. Instead Mike met some professor who's renting the cottage.'

'That's right,' Merrill said evenly. 'The cottage is mine now. I didn't want the long journey in to work each day so I let it to Professor Wendell. But. . .' She paused, frowning, then went on, 'Why should *Mike* want to see Elise?'

Luke moved back to his desk, picked up a paper-weight and stood toying with it, turning it over and over between strong, square-tipped fingers. 'You'll recall that the cheque you paid us was for a chest which we made for your cousin. When it was delivered—Rob and I took it over one evening—it looked pretty good against all the shawls and old textiles that Elise had spread around the room. I asked if we might photo-graph the chest in that setting for publicity purposes. Elise agreed, but somehow a firm date for the photography session was never fixed.'

And I know why, Merrill thought derisively. By that time you were attracted to her, and to defer the session would give you more time to get to know her. And after a while you didn't need that excuse.

Her body still clenched by the tension which had gripped her since the overwhelming surprise of Luke's reference to Elise, Merrill made a conscious effort to loosen up. 'How well did you know Elise?' she asked baldly. If Luke admitted everything, and if his rather strange manner concealed grief, however faint, then perhaps Merrill could forgive him.

'I met her only three times,' he said shortly. 'So I didn't know her very well. The first time was when she called to order the piece, and then I went to Bracken Cottage to measure——'

'*Measure*? Was that necessary?'

'In this particular case, yes.' Luke's eyebrows lifted haughtily as if surprised that Merrill should question his methods. 'She wanted it to fit as closely as possible into a particular recess. As you know, the walls of the cottage, apart from being uneven, are not vertically straight. And in the interests of doing a good job I decided to take a look at the place myself.'

Merrill glanced away lest he see the accusation in her eyes. I'll bet you did, she thought. And that was the beginning.

'And, as I said, Rob and I took the chest over when it was finished. That's when we discussed the publicity pictures. However, all that's beside the point. Mike had been ringing the cottage trying to finalise the matter while we were in Bruges. There was never a reply, and he assumed that Elise was out. So on his way to Yorkshire last Thursday evening he decided to call in and try to get things settled.'

'Well, I'm afraid photographs are out of the question now,' Merrill said firmly. 'I have the chest here in my flat in town, and all the shawls and stuff are folded up inside it. I had to clear up Elise's affairs when she died.'

Luke's face changed as he looked at her. 'You were fond of her, weren't you?' he said gently.

Surprised for the second time, Merrill nodded, swallowing the lump which had unexpectedly risen in her throat. She was astounded by the understanding in his tone. After a moment she said huskily, 'Elise was my only living relative. After she died I was alone. She was very important to me.'

'I'm sorry.' Luke frowned, went over to the coffee-machine and poured two cups, placing one in front of Merrill. 'I don't want to labour the point,' he said softly, 'but I still don't understand why the secrecy. Surely when you settled her account it would have been natural to mention her death then?'

'I—I—couldn't,' she whispered. There was a long silence as Merrill fought a desire to drop the subject which had goaded her ever since Elise died. The temptation to put aside the bitterness and suspicion was great, but, after all, she was here for only one purpose, and now Luke had given her the ideal opportunity to pursue it. She took a sip of her coffee and said, 'You seem to be making quite an issue of my not telling you, and I can't think why—especially if, as you say, you hardly knew Elise.'

'I think,' Luke said deliberately, 'that you're the one who made an issue out of it—by omission.'

Merrill closed her eyes for a moment, willing herself to hold on to her intentions. It was no good, she realised. Not by a shadow of expression, a nuance of tone, was Luke going to reveal his true involvement with Elise. Not now, probably not ever. Maybe to him Elise was dead even before she'd died. And, after having raised the subject, he was now trying to shift the emphasis away from himself by suggesting that Merrill had behaved in an unnecessarily mysterious fashion.

She stared at the rim of her cup and said tonelessly, 'As you'll have gathered, I was—devastated when I heard Elise had died. I—couldn't talk about it easily. . . She was young, vigorous, too full of life. . .' Merrill swallowed. 'Then something happened in my own private affairs that. . .' Her voice faltered for a moment, then she went on more strongly, 'Elise died in an accident. It shouldn't have happened.'

Luke nodded. 'So I heard, through Mike.

'I would have thought,' Merrill said carefully, 'that

her death would have been reported in the local newspaper——'

'It probably was. Both Mike and I were away at the time. Rob, too, I believe. As for the rest of the staff—well, I suppose to them she was just a name—another client.'

'But not to *you*?' Merrill breathed, sensing that this, at last, might be just the breakthrough she was looking for.

'Good heavens, what *are* you suggesting? Of course she was—just another client.' He stood up suddenly, sending his chair skimming back to hit the wall behind him. 'What are you implying?' he said guardedly. He seemed to tower over Merrill. 'First you make a mystery out of a fairly ordinary—although for you—tragic—event, and, believe me, I do sympathise with you over that. . . And then you seem to suggest—*what*? Just what *are* you getting at? Merrill,' he went on gravely, 'what do you know? Or, rather, what do you *think* you know?'

Merrill stood up quickly. Suddenly Luke's office seemed claustrophobic and stifling. And he hadn't even mentioned the painting which hung in his house! It was screamingly obvious that he was being less than honest about his relationship with Elise. 'Perhaps I should leave *you* to answer that question,' she whispered. 'But now, if you don't mind, I'd like to get back to my desk. I have a lot to do.'

He was watching her thoughtfully. 'All right. And perhaps,' he added grimly, 'if you keep your mind on the job you won't have time to speculate about me and——'

'Just another client?' Merrill swallowed the sob in her voice.

'Exactly,' he gritted. 'And I don't want to——' He

cut off his words abruptly as the outer door opened. 'Rob!' he exclaimed, his expression changing swiftly, 'I didn't realise you were back.'

'Oh, the proverbial bad penny, you know. . .' The young man standing in the doorway, his face healthily tanned, his brown hair sun-streaked and tousled, seemed to bring a breath of fresh air into the oppressive atmosphere. He stood looking from Luke to Merrill, then he smiled. 'I got back last night, and I'm reporting for duty.' He sketched a vague salute in Luke's direction, then his smile broadened as he looked back to Merrill. 'And just who is this?' he murmured.

Admiring blue eyes flicked over her, and his grin was so friendly and infectious that in spite of her despair Merrill felt her mouth lift a little.

'This is Merrill Stanton,' Luke said, only a faint asperity in his tone betraying the residue of his anger. 'Merrill, meet Rob, my half-brother. Of course, Rob, you knew that Alison was leaving, didn't you? Merrill is my assistant now.' He turned to her. 'You'd better get used to seeing Rob around. He'll be working with us from now on.'

'A real family firm,' Rob bantered. 'The Woodline Empire. Father would have been proud.'

Luke allowed himself a small smile then gave a brief nod in Merrill's direction. 'That'll be all for the moment,' he said. 'Oh, just make sure we're not disturbed for the next half-hour, will you?'

Rob pulled a horseshoe mouth. 'Sounds ominous,' he murmured.

As Merrill closed the door between the two offices, she heard Luke say, 'And how's Heather? I hope you managed to patch up your differences with——'

Merrill dropped into her chair. That altercation with Luke had drained her. She might have known that he would never divulge his relationship with Elise. 'Three times,' he'd said; he'd seen Elise just three times, and then purely for business reasons. But Elise's private diary spoke differently, and so did the portrait that hung in Luke's house. Proof positive that he was hiding something.

Merrill ripped a sheet of paper from her typewriter with an angry, protesting sound, and, gritting her teeth, turned back to her notes. She would do her job—and do it well right until the very day when she left the company. Her motive in taking up this particular post had no purpose now that she realised that Luke would never go back on his story. Somehow, once again, she'd handled the situation badly. She should have known that she couldn't outwit him!

As she plodded through her notes she decided that at the end of the month she would hand in her notice, and on the day she left she would brandish Elise's diary before his eyes. Vindictive, yes, but no more than he deserved, and worth the moral cost to herself just for the pleasure of exposing him.

Lunch-hour came and went, but with Merrill's stomach still churning she was in no mood to eat. It was almost two o'clock when her door opened and Rob looked round. 'Good heavens.' he said sunnily, 'he *does* work you hard!'

'Mmm?' Merrill looked up vaguely, then glanced at her watch. 'I had no idea of the time,' she murmured, pushing back a tendril of hair and leaning back in her chair.

'I thought we ought to get better acquainted, seeing as we're all part of this happy family. Had lunch?' Rob's eyebrows lifted enquiringly. 'No, I thought not. Come on, then. Big Brother's gone off somewhere, and——'

'No, I won't, thank you. I've got——'

'Tons to do? I know. Luke told me to leave you alone. But I'm sure that even he wouldn't want you to starve; it might affect your output,' he laughed. 'I won't take no for an answer. Now come along. At least have a coffee and a sandwich. Otherwise you'll be passing out by five o'clock.'

Merrill gave him the ghost of a grin. 'Masterful, aren't you?'

'Like all the Travis men,' Rob answered complacently. 'It accounts for our success with women.'

'You don't have to tell me,' Merrill murmured. Then she smiled again. 'All right, I accept your offer. Thank you.' A little of the gloom was lifting from her spirits now that Luke was out of the office.

'I'm surprised you don't take lunch with Mike's secretary,' Rob remarked, holding open the door.

'Kate? Oh, she's got a boyfriend home on leave from somewhere or other, and they meet for lunch. . .' Merrill hugged her jacket around her more closely as they turned into the wind and crossed the road to a small wine bar.

'And you? Don't you have a boyfriend to take you out to lunch?' Rob asked idly, with a sideways glance at the cloud of dark hair streaming behind her. 'You should have.'

Merrill smiled. 'Don't you think that's a rather personal question at this point? After all, this morning I barely knew of your existence. But,' she added drily, 'if you're curious about my private life, why not ask Luke? I believe he thinks he has the answers.'

'Oh, far be it from me to pry,' Rob said loftily, 'I was merely paying you an indirect compliment.' He held the door open for her then followed her into the warmth of the bar. 'And don't be alarmed, I'm not trying to score. As a matter of fact,' he added confidentially, drawing out a chair for her, 'I got engaged while I was in Cortina.'

'Congratulations,' Merrill said. 'But—a holiday romance? Was that wise? They're not always to be trusted in the long term, you know.'

'You're beginning to sound like Luke,' Rob grinned. 'Don't tell me he's brain-washed you already. . . Practical and sensible, warning me away from magic, all that stuff. But you've got it wrong. I've known Heather for quite a while—a sort of on-and-off relationship, I suppose. But I came to my senses and declared my honourable intentions at the top of Mount Pocol.'

'How very romantic!' Merrill clasped her hands and stared at him with softly humourous eyes. This seemed to be the kind of light, bantering conversation that Rob invited.

'Yes, it was rather. Then I kissed her. Then I skied down.'

'And, naturally, Heather followed you,' Merrill prompted gently.

'What else?' Rob's laughter rang out in the cosy room, the faint white lines around his eyes wrinkling against his winter tan. 'Of course, it isn't official yet. I'm waiting until my mother gets back from her cruise.' He took a sip of wine, studying Merrill smilingly. 'I reckon you'd like Heather. Everyone does. Luke thinks there's no one to touch her.'

'Really?' Merrill couldn't keep the sharpness out of her voice at the mention of Luke's name. 'Is he jealous, then?'

'Heavens, no! He just thinks Heather is a real cracker, and it's time I settled down. Doesn't that sound dreary? Enough to put anyone off!'

'And is that the reason you're marrying her? Because

she has Luke's seal of approval?' Carefully Merrill removed the cress garnish from her sandwich.

'Oh, nothing like that. . . No, it's just that. . .well, I suppose I've played around quite a lot. Funny, though, I always came back to Heather. But now,' he went on thoughtfully, 'I find that playing around isn't much fun any more. I've learned what I want. And Luke's liking Heather is a bonus, I suppose. So,' he went on, 'when Ma gets back we'll be throwing a big engagement party. It'll have to be at Luke's place—my flat's too small. So you'll come.' He grinned again, obviously used to getting his own way. 'And I'm sure that Luke——' He stopped suddenly, looking beyond Merrill's face. 'Well, talk of the devil!' he exclaimed. He stood up. 'Come and join us, Luke. I'm just telling Merrill my momentous news.'

Apparently impervious to Luke's quick frown, he drew up another chair. 'I've just invited her to my engagement party,' he added.

'Oh. . . Thank you, but I—I don't know,' Merrill demurred, trying to quell the panic that fluttered inside her at Luke's unexpected appearance.

Luke smiled urbanely. 'Perhaps Merrill will have other arrangements,' he murmured, summoning the waiter.

Rob laughed. 'Then she can bring him with her.' He winked at Merrill. 'The more the merrier.'

'Well,' Merrill said weakly, 'we'll think about that when the time comes.'

Rob glanced at Luke. 'I didn't expect to see you here,' he remarked. 'This place isn't one of your usual haunts.'

Luke made a non-committal noise, and suddenly Merrill had the impression that he had guessed she would be here with Rob.

Throughout the rest of the uncomfortable meal she was aware of his speculative glance. His presence inhibited her, completely destroying the pleasant atmosphere which had prevailed between Rob and herself, and after a few moments she took no part in the talk, merely listening with interest to Rob's account of his holiday.

As soon as she had finished her coffee she stood up. 'Thank you for the lunch, Rob,' she smiled, 'but I ought to get back now.'

'Yes,' Luke said, 'perhaps you should.' His eyes were hard as he watched her draw on her gloves; clearly he was still angry with her. 'I'd like that report this afternoon, if possible. I need to take immediate action. . . And there are a couple of letters that must go off today.' Although his tone was courteous, his words were a pointed reminder of her position.

'The pleasure was all mine,' Rob said, acknowledging Merrill's thanks. 'We'll do it again some time.'

'Don't bank on it,' Luke interposed, before Merrill could speak. 'I intend to keep your nose to the grindstone, Rob. As a potential breadwinner, you'd better start concentrating on your career, and not——'

Not flirt with the hired help, Merrill wanted to add, but as Rob winked conspiratorially at her she smiled. At least *he* was prepared to be amiable and friendly, and that would make office life a lot more pleasant during her remaining weeks with Woodline Design.

CHAPTER SIX

DURING the following days it became apparent to Merrill that not only did Luke mean to keep Rob's nose well and truly to the grindstone, but he didn't intend to take the pressure off her either—although, in fairness, she had to admit that Luke worked harder than both of them. So, when Saturday dawned, it was with a feeling of release that she threw her wetsuit into the car and drove to the sailing club.

She had quickly learned the rudiments of windsurfing, and her instructor told her that she was a 'natural'. She had spent more than she intended on the wetsuit, but couldn't resist its bright fuchsia colours. Today she intended to apply to join the sailing club and, hopefully, find herself a second-hand sailboard.

The spring day was unseasonably warm, and after two hour's tuition she went into the clubhouse. Her instructor had given her the name of a boy who was selling a sailboard and who would be here in time for the afternoon race.

So she waited, pleasantly relaxed after an exhilarating morning, idly watching the buoys being laid to mark the course of the race, and wondering when she would be confident enough to take part.

In one corner of the clubhouse a group of children were obviously waiting for someone, and behind the bar the steward polished glasses busily. Merrill sat back, enjoying the warmth of the sun through the large glass windows.

A sudden voice behind her startled her, and she

turned sharply. 'I'd know you anywhere—even from the back, and wearing an exotic wetsuit at that,' Luke said.

Merrill blinked, wishing that the hot colour hadn't flooded her face. She probably looked like a guilty schoolgirl caught out in some prank. And that was ridiculous; she had every right to be here.

'Oh, hello,' she murmured lamely. 'I didn't expect to see *you*!'

'Or you wouldn't have come,' Luke supplied calmly.

'Yes, I would. I'm applying for membership, and I'm hoping to buy a sailboard this afternoon,' she retorted, and blushed again.

This is *ridiculous*, she told herself, maddened by her reaction. With an effort she pulled her gaze away from the tall figure clad in blue trousers and black T-shirt. A cream sweater was knotted by its sleeves around his neck. He looked very casual and exactly right. Aware of her figure-hugging wetsuit, she shifted uncomfortably in her chair.

'Then I'll see that your membership application gets processed quickly,' Luke murmured. 'May I join you?' He was pulling out a chair. 'Oh, in case you didn't know, I'm the commodore of the club. Yes,' he smiled, seeing her disbelief, 'it's true. Haven't you read the list of officers on the notice board?'

'No,' Merrill said. 'I've been coming as a mere visitor. I never gave it a glance.'

'Let me get you another coffee,' Luke offered, then added, 'That is, if you're alone.' As she nodded, he went on, 'But first. . .' He got up and walked over to the group of children and chatted with them for a moment. Merrill watched him covertly, wondering if she would have had the courage to sit here if she had known that he would come in; wondering if she would have joined another and more distant club had she known that he was the commodore here.

She saw him go to the bar and order a tray of Cokes and crisps for the children, and by the time he came back to her table carrying two mugs of coffee she had composed herself a little.

'Small world, isn't it?' he said softly. 'I didn't know that you were a watersports enthusiast.'

'Oh, I'm still a very raw novice. And I didn't know *you* were.'

He laughed. 'I once had ideas of sailing around the world, doing a Sir Francis Chichester, you know, but work got in the way, and I had to lower my sights.'

Merrill looked at him questioningly. 'But don't you ever feel like—well, just packing everything in and just—going? I mean, if it was an ambition, a dream. . .?'

'I thought about it occasionally, but. . .' he shrugged, raising one eyebrow '. . .Family responsibilities, people depending upon one—you know how it goes.'

'No, I don't really,' Merrill said, thinking of her own lonely state.

'No, of course not. Sorry. So,' he went on with the air of finalising the subject, 'I've narrowed my horizons.' He drained his cup and stood up.

'Are you racing this afternoon?' Merrill asked.

He shook his head and glanced over to the children. 'I'm giving some instruction. I might see you later, then?'

'I doubt it. I'm simply waiting to see a man about a sailboard, then I shall go home.'

'Pity. I could have taken you out in my dinghy.' There was a challenging glint in his eyes, and he was smiling crookedly. 'Would you have come?' he asked, softly taunting.

Merrill shook her head quickly, confused by his words. 'Sorry,' she said, 'but I haven't the time.'

'No, of course not. I was forgetting your chock-a-bloc social diary,' he said smoothly. 'Have fun, then. As if you needed telling. . .' He turned away, beckoning the children, and they trooped out behind him.

Merrill watched them walk across to where a group of small dinghies was moored. From what she could see, he was showing the children how to rig the boats. There seemed to be a lot of laughter and some mild horseplay.

The steward came to stand beside her. 'It's good that they can come here,' he murmured, looking out at the lively group. Then in answer to Merrill's raised eyebrows, 'They're from one of the children's homes. Mr Travis gives a lot of time to the kids, not to mention buying those five Toppers for them to learn in. Generous, wasn't it?'

'Y-yes,' Merrill said thoughtfully. 'Very generous indeed.' And, she would have added, the last thing she'd have expected of him. She frowned; Luke was certainly full of surprises.

'You're looking a little fragile,' Rob remarked the following Monday, as he perched on her desk.

'I'm busy, that's all,' Merrill murmured. 'I got a whole morning off in Bruges, and I guess I've been making up for it ever since.'

Rob laughed. 'Well, what do you expect as personal assistant to a workaholic? Didn't he warn you that it would be no bed of roses? Still, I don't know why you put up with it. I'm sure you could find yourself a nice easy job where you don't have to do much apart from

enhance the décor. And you would do that very well,'
he said with a mock-leer.

'Flatterer!' Merrill stapled a batch of papers
together. 'Still, it won't be for long. . .' She stopped
before she revealed her future plans. 'I mean, once I
get this analysis out of the way things might——' She
stopped again as Luke appeared in the doorway.

'Nothing to do, Rob?' he enquired pleasantly.
'Good. Then perhaps you can give me your opinion on
some stained glass designs.' His gaze moved to Merrill.
'Finished the analysis yet?'

'Almost.' It was hard to reconcile this crisp, terse
executive with the casual shorts-clad figure she had last
seen on the jetty of the sailing club, directing the noisy,
giggling group of children.

And workaholic was the right word, she thought,
after Rob had gone out. Luke seemed to lose no
opportunity of parting her and Rob whenever he found
them together, as if he couldn't bear to see them
slacken pace. Then Merrill paused, her hands idle on
the keyboard. Or might he have other motives? Did
his opinion of her prompt him to try to scotch any
possibility of a friendship developing between Rob and
herself?

Merrill sighed. It seemed feasible. By Luke's own
admission he saw her as shallow, someone interested
only in a good time and a string of boyfriends. Did he,
then, believe that she might present a threat to Rob's
engagement—to a girl he liked and approved of?

Oh, forget it! Merrill told herself. Why should I
waste my time pondering over Luke's motives—for
anything?

She leaned back, straightening her spine and stretching. In a sense the recent pressure of work was a
blessing, for it isolated her, forcing her to concentrate

so intensely that she simply had no time to dig deeply into such perplexities.

Just after five o'clock she took the correspondence into his office for signature. He had already cleared his desk and was obviously ready to leave. She watched the gold pen glide over the paper, then he handed the letters back to her for posting.

'You've been working extremely hard.' He put his pen away, watching her inscrutably.

'So you've noticed?' she murmured. 'Well, I can't say you didn't warn me.'

'Right. But even so. . .since we got back from Belgium things here have been hectic, even by *my* exacting standards.'

'Well, I intend to give myself a reward,' Merrill said, going over to his window and closing it. 'A long, hot, luxurious bath, a quick, no-fuss freezer supper, and an early night.'

He raised one eyebrow, a quizzical tilt to his mouth. 'That sounds madly over-the-top. Why not the luxurious et cetera bath, and let *me* take you out to a *decent* dinner?'

Merrill turned to stare at him. He had to be joking! After the atmosphere that sparked between them whenever they spent a few hours together. . .! He was watching her challengingly now, a goading light in his eyes. Slowly she sealed an envelope as he put on his coat. 'You're not serious,' she murmured after a moment.

'Never more so.' He had reached the door. He opened it and said over his shoulder, 'I'll call for you at seven-thirty. All right?'

Then he was gone, and Merrill was left staring wide-eyed after him, the sheaf of letters frozen in her hands.

What consummate arrogance! She had spoken of a

reward, not a *penance*! Of course, she wouldn't go; the image of him standing in the porch of the tall house, pressing the bell pointlessly, made her lips twitch. I shall run my bath at seven twenty-five precisely, she decided, and I won't even hear him when he calls. Forcefully she thrust her arms into the sleeves of her jacket, anxious to be away from the place.

Her car was having one of its bad days, and it was some twenty minutes before the engine fired success-fully. Merrill had known that the battery needed replacing, and with no special plans in view this seemed as good a time as any to get it done.

By the time a new battery had been fitted, and she had wasted some more minutes with a mechanic who appeared not to want to go home, it was twenty past six before Merrill reached her flat.

The incident with the car had taken her mind off Luke, but as she changed into a housecoat a sudden idea flashed across her mind. Of course! she could see it all now: Luke had suggested this date to give him the opportunity to warn her off Rob! There could be no other reason. He *must* be worried! She laughed aloud; what lengths he was prepared to go to, just to issue a veto which wasn't in the least necessary.

She removed the wrapping from her supper, then stopped, biting her lip thoughtfully, tempted to lead Luke on a little, to let him worry. After all, why should he get away with everything? And why should he assume that he alone had the power to manipulate others? He had dodged the issue over Elise, and he had labelled her, Merrill, as a fly-by-night, so why shouldn't he pay for it?

Hastily she pushed the food into the fridge, then went into the bathroom and turned on the taps, pouring in the expensive bath essence that she hadn't used since her London days when Max had played such a big part in her life. How curious that she could now think of him without the tiniest pang; it was as if the shadow of Max had been totally eclipsed by the substance of Luke—with all its ramifications.

Oddly, she didn't feel at all tired now. In fact, stimulated by the prospect ahead, she found that she was looking forward to the evening. She smiled at her reflection in the steamy mirror. *This* I'm going to enjoy, she told herself.

When Luke called her heart seemed to expand at the look of admiration that slipped over his face as his gaze took in her simple cream suit in thick, crunchy lace, the severe black camisole she wore beneath it, but he merely murmured, 'Punctual as always. I must say, I do like that in my women.'

'*Your* women?' Then, when he didn't answer, something egged her on. 'But punctuality wasn't one of Elise's virtues.'

He gave a quick frown. 'No? Well, I wouldn't know about that. But suppose we drop the subject of Elise for this evening? It seems a rather clouded issue.'

'Oh, of course,' Merrill smiled, settling herself luxuriously in the car. 'Anything you say. Where are we going?'

'To a new place. It opened only this month, and already it's noted for its cuisine and cellar.'

'Oh, *good*. I'm absolutely ravenous,' she said brightly.

'And there's more. Do you like dancing?'

Just in time she stopped herself from confiding that she'd almost forgotten how to dance.

'That depends on my partner,' she hedged.

He laughed. 'I've been practising.'

Merrill couldn't stop her own laughter at the picture

his words conjured up. Whatever else Luke was—and, heaven knew, he had so many facets—he could be great company when he chose.

'Did you see the man about the sailboard?' he asked as they left the town limits behind.

'Yes, and I bought it. And how did you get on with the children?'

She heard the smile in his voice. 'It was par for the course. Two of them succeeded in capsizing their dinghies. They do it on purpose; it adds to the excitement, and I shouldn't think they get much of that.'

'Didn't it worry you?'

'No. They were wearing life-jackets, and I was there, of course. Besides, I don't take them into deep water. Having a spill gives them a thrill, and it's something for them to talk about afterwards.'

'It's very good of you to do it,' Merrill said slowly.

He nodded complacently. 'Well, I'm a good guy.' He laughed dismissively.

'Generous, too. I understand that you provided the dinghies.'

'Someone's been telling tales. . . I can afford it. Didn't we land a big contract in Bruges? Now enough of these compliments, Merrill, or you'll turn my head. Besides, you're acting out of character. And don't scowl now; you know it's true.'

A few moments later he pulled into the gravelled forecourt of a large house.

'Call this *new*?' Merrill asked, staring up at the mellowed golden stone of the Elizabethan house, floodlit among its setting of ancient trees.

'I meant—it's newly opened as a night spot.'

'Well, I think it's lovely,' she said later as she touched the crisp carving of the linenfold panelling by their table.

'I'm glad you approve.' He looked up from the menu he was studying and smiled suddenly. Merrill felt her heart tilt as he said softly, 'But the setting does no more than justice to the subject.'

She glanced down quickly, conscious of the heightened beat of her blood. Oh, if only he were different! But not *completely* different, an inner voice amended doggedly. She smothered a sigh; why couldn't it be straightforward? At this very moment it was difficult to hold on to her reservations about him; difficult and almost impossible not to fit in and go along with his present mood and be more than happy to do so.

At last, their order given, he took a sip of his very dry sherry and said, 'This reminds me of that evening we spent together in Bruges—except that your hair was done differently then, and you wore a deep-pink dress.'

'Watermelon-pink,' she defined. 'But I'm surprised that you remembered that detail.'

'You don't forget the unforgettable,' he said, so softly that for a moment Merrill wondered if she had heard him correctly. She stared down into her sherry glass, a confusion of warmth mounting inside her. 'Still,' he added, 'you'll have heard that kind of compliment often enough, I'm sure.'

Was that a reaffirmation of his opinion of her? 'But never *too* often,' she said airily, wondering how one countered a remark of that kind.

'Then I'll make a point of repeating it—at five-minute intervals.'

She laughed. 'Why all this sweetness and light?' she asked wryly. 'You don't *have* to work at it, you know.'

'Who's talking about work? This is sheer, unadulterated pleasure. Ah, our table's ready.'

He took her arm as they went into the dining-room.

His touch burned like a brand through the cream lace, and somewhere at her core a traitorous butterfly-like tremor began. And this time wine played no part in it.

In an effort to bring herself down to earth again, she said pleasantly, 'You never told me how you got into Woodline Design. I mean, are you there simply because it's a family business, or would you have done it anyway?'

He watched her over the rim of his glass, his eyes lambent, his mouth uptilted. 'You want to talk about *me*?' he taunted softly. 'What man could resist such an invitation?'

She stifled the admission that they had to talk about something—anything—to take her mind off the contradictory emotions that stirred inside her, and managed a casual shrug. 'Not many, I suspect.'

He laughed suddenly, his eyes crinkling to points of amber light, his teeth a flash of white. It gave him a rakish, devil-may-care look completely at variance with his austere manner of recent days. 'All right, Merrill, you've asked for it.'

He went on to talk lightly and amusingly of his training, touching on his early failures. To Merrill, he became more human by the minute as her imagination pictured Luke, the boy, then Luke in his early twenties trying to harness his self-confessed high-flown ideas to the practicalities of his craft. 'And of course,' he concluded, 'I had my father. He was my mentor. After my mother died, and he married Stella—well, even then, with a new marriage, his support and guidance never faltered.'

'So you were very close,' Merrill murmured. His story had been absorbing and very revealing; it was difficult to relate it to the other, more menacing side of him.

He nodded. 'Yes, very close.'

'I'm sure he would be proud of you,' Merrill said slowly, still marvelling at this new-found empathy. 'You've carried on his life's work, and added to it your own interpretation of the skills he taught you.'

'You *are* complimentary tonight!' he said, very softly. Then, as if sensing her confusion, he went on, 'Now, how about you? Of course, when we were in Bruges you told me about the hypochondriac darling you worked for, but what about before that?'

Merrill toyed with her cheese-knife, and when she spoke her voice was slightly breathless. Somehow that reference to Bruges had thrown her a little. 'Well,' she said hurriedly, 'I *didn't* carry on the family business. As I've told you, my father was a landscape architect, and my mother started a small business growing herbs and old-fashioned roses to start with. Eventually it blossomed into a garden centre. I used to help at weekends and during school holidays. But when my parents—died, it was sold. It didn't make us rich, and it was hard work, but it seemed a kind of—good, worthwhile occupation—growing things. . .'

She hesitated, but Luke nodded as if he understood perfectly. Merrill dabbed her mouth with the big damask napkin and put it down. 'So now,' she concluded, 'I'm trying to bring some order and beauty to the garden at the back of my flat, as you know. That, too, seems worthwhile: each week some little neglected plant that's survived the lack of attention pops up.'

'Funny,' he said. 'If I hadn't seen you struggling with that dandelion I wouldn't have said you were the muddy-boots type.'

'Ah, well, if it comes to that,' Merrill smiled, trying to dispel an atmosphere of gathering intimacy that seemed to be waiting in the wings, 'I've never imagined you actually sharpening chisels and tramping about in sawdust.'

'*Touché*,' he murmured. Smoothly he leaned across the table, his hand capturing her own. The dreaded, wonderful thrill came back, starting at the base of Merrill's spine and quivering up to her throat. Her eyes widened suddenly in protest, and she tried to withdraw her hand, but his light grip tightened. 'Perhaps,' he said softly, 'there's a lot that we both have to learn about each other. Now might be a good time to begin. Let's start with coffee in the other room.'

'It was a delicious meal,' Merrill said politely. 'Thank you.'

'When Sam and Anna come over, I think I'll bring them here,' he remarked idly. 'I enjoyed it, too. With Stella away I'm having to fend for myself. I'm not much of a cook.' His hand reached for hers again as they went into what might have been a salon in the heyday of the old house. Small groups of chairs and tables were lit by rose-shaded lamps around an intimate dance-floor. In one corner a trio played easy, romantic music. When the tiny coffee-cups were cleared, Luke said with a smile, 'Well? Shall we?'

Going into his arms, Merrill's body seemed to melt. He held her closely, not talking, and she was grateful for the silence so that she could just *be*. Their rapport strengthened in a myriad sensations. This, Merrill decided dizzily, was the most perfect of evenings.

When the music stopped they looked at each other for a long moment, then reluctantly drew apart. The light and often humorous tone of the evening had changed completely into a silence charged with something heavier, potent and compelling.

They danced again, then Luke said a little hoarsely, 'Shall we go?'

Wordlessly, Merrill nodded. Their fingers were linked as they walked to the car, but her body clamoured for more. She hoped that he would stop and kiss her, but he didn't.

Of course he didn't! Like her, he had been influenced by the insidious trapping of romance: the place, the meal, the music, the whole ambience. And now, like her, he was recalling the object of the evening's exercise!

Oh, it was all so shabby! Merrill thought, as she sat in the car as far away as possible from him. So false—all that carefully orchestrated intimacy. But now reality, cold and uncompromising, was back. . . Luke, the man who had such a low opinion of her and who had contrived this date presumably to serve his own devious ends, this man who had denied—yes, even earlier tonight—any involvement with Elise. . . And herself, mistrustful of him, angered by his wrong assumptions about her, pretending to go along with the programme he'd arranged! Small wonder that her emotions had see-sawed.

He, too, was quiet during the drive back, but as he pulled in outside her flat he said thoughtfully, as if they were continuing a conversation, 'Of course, some guys get invited up for coffee.'

'Do they? I wonder why?' she mused.

'You could try it and find out,' he murmured.

Well, why not? she asked herself. She wasn't likely to become enchanted for the second time this evening—her common sense would see to that. Besides, a refusal would seem as if she placed too much importance on an accepted practice. Anyway it would be interesting to learn just at what point he would get around to the subject of Rob.

'Please sit down,' she said formally, a moment later, 'while I make the coffee.'

It wasn't going to be that easy; her flat—previously her haven from Luke and the bafflement and anger which he had always aroused in her—now seemed to vibrate with his presence. His essential force pervaded every corner of the high room, dominating it. Not that that was unusual; hadn't he always dominated whatever space he was in?

Piercingly aware of his presence in the next room, her hand shook as she spooned coffee into the filter cup and switched on the machine. Absently she watched the milk heat in the pan, saw the faint shiver on the surface as a skin threatened to form. Quickly she snatched the pan from the hotplate, but the handle caught in her sleeve, and, in trying to correct the balance and stop the lace from tearing, she burned her thumb.

'Something wrong?' Luke was beside her in response to her small, involuntary squeal. He propelled her over to the sink and turned on the cold tap, holding her hand beneath it.

'That was clumsy of me,' Merrill murmured.

'Got a bandage—just to keep the air out?'

Merrill nodded, oblivious now to the fire in her thumb. His nearness eclipsed all other sensations. She wondered miserably just how much more she could take of this inner desperation. 'In that drawer,' she said weakly.

Deftly Luke bandaged her hand. 'Go and sit down. I can, at least, make coffee.'

Thankfully Merrill escaped, glad of an opportunity to try and get herself together again. She sank down on to the sofa, breathing deeply to steady herself. This evening hadn't gone to plan. Just where—and when, and how—had it begun to go astray? At what moment had she surrendered the tactics she'd planned to the charismatic persuasion of Luke's personality?

But there was no time to work that out for he was back in the room, carrying a tray, and with his foot hooking forward the coffee-table.

'All right now?' he asked, nodding towards her hand.

Flustered, she laughed. 'It's nothing. A bit fiery, but don't worry—I'll still be able to type.'

'It may surprise you to hear that typing is the last thing on my mind,' he said softly, sitting down beside her.

Damn, she thought, why didn't I choose a chair?

He moved smoothly, almost imperceptibly. She felt his arm across her shoulders drawing her towards him. His other hand cupped her chin, tilting her face upwards so that there was no escape from the gaze that held her own, trapping her in a world which only the two of them knew. There was only his mouth—relaxed, sensual—the intent in his eyes, the faint, elusive fragrance of his cologne. . .

Very slowly his head moved. He was still looking into her eyes and his mouth found her parted lips. And all the sensations he had aroused tonight, and in Bruges, flooded back, drowning everything but Merrill's own desire. His lips seemed to draw out from her all that was sweet, all that was female, and she gave herself up to the moment with an abandon that shocked her.

Slowly his mouth released hers as he held her against him, the movement of his breath stirring her hair. 'I've wanted this so often,' he breathed. 'When you've looked at me coldly—as you so often have—I've wanted to warm you, melt you. When you've tried to hide your anger, I've wanted to kiss it to death. Merrill. . . Oh, Merrill. . .'

His mouth captured hers again with a strength and intent that made her gasp. She felt his hands move, his fingers sensuously stroking her breasts, refuelling those kiss-fired desires. She had intuitively sensed that his effect would be devastating. Now she *knew*. The sensations she had experienced in Bruges were mere *frissons* compared with this storm of need. . . How had she managed to survive the intervening weeks when this was what she was made for?

His fingertips feathered her nipples, and she heard his smothered exclamation of pleasure at their stiff thrust as he bent his head to scatter random kisses down the line of her throat. When he lifted his head, she saw that his eyes were dark with desire. His mouth commanded hers again, as if he would never let her go, and his tongue was an exquisite torment. 'More, darling. . .' he whispered. 'There's more. . . Let me show you. Let me love you——'

The shrill of the telephone cut cruelly across his words. For a moment Merrill's enchantment seemed to hang in suspension, then she sat up quickly, pushing back her hair.

'Leave it,' he gritted hoarsely. 'Let the damn thing ring.'

'I—I can't. Diane—the girl in the next flat—is expecting a call from the hospital. It may be important. . .'

'Hell,' Luke growled disgustedly, 'that's just what we need—your neighbour dropping in.'

But it wasn't the hospital. Instead, Rob's cheerful tones came over the wire. 'Luke there? I thought he might be. He said he was taking you out tonight. Sorry to break up the party, but——'

Merrill didn't wait to hear the rest. Silently, and still bemused, she held out the receiver. Dimly she heard Luke's terse voice as he spoke.

Rob. What perfect timing. Merrill bit her lip. In a few more moments this love scene would have reached the point of no return. She wanted to weep for the ecstasy she would never know now.

She stood up and carried the cold coffee into the kitchen. She smoothed her hair and straightened the shoulder-straps of her black camisole, then with an effort composed her face into an expression of detached amusement as she went back into the other room. 'Well,' she said seeing that Luke was no longer on the phone, 'so it was Rob, after all. Aren't you pleased I insisted on answering?'

She saw Luke's face change, grow baffled, then harden as he noted her composure. 'His car's broken down. He wants me to give Heather a lift home.' He paused for a moment, then, 'I'm so sorry,' he added urbanely.

Merrill moved away from the kitchen doorway. 'Don't apologise,' she said with a short laugh. 'These things happen, don't they?' She bent to plump up the cushions. 'I like Rob, you know.'

'Yes, I'd gathered that.'

At a stroke Luke's tone confirmed Merrill's earlier suspicions about his motives in asking her to dine with him.

'I could have done without this tonight,' Luke said. 'And they *could* have arranged for a taxi.'

'Oh, I expect they're saving hard for their wedding,' Merrill said carelessly. 'I would have thought such good sense would have met with your approval.' Absently she twitched a fading tulip from its vase and dropped it into the waste-paper basket. 'You're very pleased about their engagement, I believe? I find that rather surprising, considering that you appear to find bachelor status the answer.'

Luke leaned back slightly, resting his hands on the edge of the telephone-table behind him. He was watching her closely, his brow creased in concentration. After a moment, he said warily, 'The answer to what? I wasn't aware of any problem. Shall we just say that I didn't meet the right woman? Also, I have my work, in case you hadn't noticed.'

They were well and truly entrenched in the old animosity now, Merrill thought. 'Yes, I *had* noticed,' she murmured. 'But somehow I get the impression that Rob isn't so deeply committed to the company as you are. He still seems to have time for—fun. And why not? He's a very attractive man.'

She knew that she was goading Luke, but, recalling her earlier intentions, why not? Let him worry a little. He simply could not go around labelling people, and moving them about as if they were chess pieces, just to suit his own ends.

Luke's face darkened perceptibly. 'I'm sure you're not alone in that opinion.' He shrugged himself upright and moved towards the door. 'However, it seems that Rob's come to his senses at last and realised that Heather is the only person he wants. So I doubt if he'll provide much—*fun* for anyone else,' he added significantly.

And that's what you've been wanting to say all evening, Merrill thought: a nice, discreet 'keep off' instruction.

'Why, Luke,' she exclaimed softly, 'it sounds as if you're warning me off!'

He spun round, his mouth grim. 'Just in case it's necessary,' he clipped out.

'And that's why you took me out tonight?' Merrill smiled gently. 'Thank you. Maybe I should even feel a little flattered that you consider me sufficiently important to be a threat to Rob's engagement.'

It seemed incredible now that Luke had held her in those heart-rocking moments, that the hands which were now thrust deeply into his pockets had caressed her until she was torn with longing.

'No,' he ground out. 'That was *not* the reason!'

'Oh, come on, Luke!' Merrill never knew how she managed the careless, amused laugh. 'Why not be honest—for once? Whenever you've seen Rob in my office you've taken good care to get him out of my clutches very smartly, on the flimsiest of pretexts. Do you think I haven't noticed? You're pleased about his engagement—he told me that some time ago—and you've as good as admitted it tonight.' She tucked a stray curl behind her ear. 'So you see me as something of a threat,' she mused, then shrugged. 'Natural enough, I suppose, considering you have me black-listed as—how shall I put it?—something of a predator.'

'Look here——' He took a sudden step forward, his features tight with rage. 'Just a minute——'

'No. *You* look. . . Aren't you being a little old-fashioned? Hasn't it occurred to you that in today's harsh world it's every girl for herself? If we want something, then we go for it in the best possible way we know. What else can we do? We live in a very competitive age.' She paused for a moment, forcing herself to meet his narrowed gaze. 'We don't all wait around any more, like wallflowers at a dance, hoping that the man we fancy will deign to notice us. And we don't necessarily feel overwhelmed with gratitude if he does.'

'What the hell are you talking about?' Luke sparked.

'Isn't it obvious?' Merrill marvelled at the pitying note in her voice. 'I'm talking about *me*, of course. And you. And perhaps Rob. For as *I'm* still a free agent perhaps your veto should be directed at *him*. After all, he's the person you're concerned about.'

The anger in Luke's face had deepened while she had been speaking. Well, wasn't that what she had wanted—to let him see that she had known all along what lay behind his invitation this evening? And it was even more important that he should see, also, that she hadn't been deflected by persuasive words and looks, kisses that seemed to draw her soul from her body. It would, she concluded unhappily, have been better for her own peace of mind if he hadn't gone to such extreme lengths, but as he had. . . 'No,' she went on coolly, 'don't waste your time trying to warn me off Rob. Oh, I admit it was rather clever of you to engineer that intimate little scene we've just shared, but *I* wasn't fooled. Not for one moment.'

She'd had enough now. Why didn't he just go while she could still maintain some degree of composure, this deliberate distancing of herself from the rapture that had possessed her before the telephone rang?

Luke scowled savagely. 'Are you *really* suggesting that——'

'Yes, I am. I saw through it, you know. I guessed it was part of your plot to steer me right away from Rob—in case I corrupt him.' She gave a tinkling little laugh. 'You'd hoped that after a love scene with you I'd have no further interest in Rob. Oh, Luke,' she chided gently, 'what conceit! You should never under-estimate a woman's intuition, you know.'

'You mean you—really—think that——'

'Wasn't that your motive in asking me out? To soften

me up for the kill? I can think of no other reason. After all, it's patently obvious than we don't get along together most of the time.'

For a moment they faced each other, frozen in hostility. Then Luke wiped the anger from his face in a blandness that smoothed his brow and relaxed the tight mouth. He swung his car keys carelessly. 'All right, Merrill. Perhaps I *did* underestimate your intelligence.'

He turned then, and opened the door, saying over his shoulder, 'But it *almost* worked, didn't it? In fact,' he added with silken cruelty, 'I would have put money on it working, they way things were going. That is, until the telephone rang.'

Then he was gone. A few moments later Merrill heard his car start, then roar away into the night.

The tears which she had, by a superhuman effort, held in check, now rose, and with impatient fingers she brushed them away angrily. What a cold-blooded devil he was! And what monumental arrogance—to think that an evening in his company would be enough to wean her away from Rob—that was if she had been interested in Rob in the first place!

Well, she had only herself to blame, she thought, trying to be philosophical. Tonight she had come full circle—from merely suspecting Luke's motives to hearing him finally admit them.

Her body still seemed to hold the imprint of his hands, her lips remembered his—firm, warm, promising, exciting. . . How *did* one forget feelings like that? she asked herself bleakly. But there was no answer.

Wearily she undressed, then stepped into the shower. Her body was still fragrant from her earlier bath, but now in a frenzy of haste she was desperate to rinse it off—all of it: the perfume and the caresses— ashes of a fire with which she had stupidly played.

CHAPTER SEVEN

'WHAT's eating Big Brother this morning?' Rob asked with a grimace the following day. He had come into Merrill's office ostensibly for paper-clips, and now he stood with his back towards her, staring out of the window on to the rain-swept traffic below. 'His expression is just about as dreary as the weather.'

'Is it? I hadn't really noticed,' Merrill answered indifferently. She was in no mood to discuss Luke's expression, nor anything else about him. His manner had been exaggeratedly polite and impersonal when they had opened the mail together earlier. He had made no mention of the previous evening, nor had she expected him to. Obviously he was the kind of man who could expunge an unsatisfactory incident from his memory as if it had never happened, and get on with living in the present.

The edges of Merrill's mind felt frayed. She toyed uncertainly with the idea of handing in her resignation today. What was the point in punishing herself unnecessarily by continuing to work in such a hostile atmosphere, no matter how interesting the actual job was? Being used—as Luke had used her last night— was humiliating, and even though she had been able to turn the tables it had left a bitter after-taste.

She went on typing, only half listening to Rob's grumbles, until he said suddenly, 'Have lunch with me, Merrill?'

She stiffened but didn't answer immediately, pretending to study her notes with fixed concentration.

Rob came over to perch on the corner of her desk. 'What have I done?' he asked. 'Are you angry with me because I phoned Luke at your place last night? Was it the wrong moment?'

She shook her head, flipping over the pages of her notebook. If you only knew, she thought—it was exactly the *right* moment.

'Well, then,' he went on, 'much as I enjoy looking at the top of your head, I did ask a question. So what about it? Lunch?'

'Don't crowd me, Rob.' Merrill got up and crossed to the stationery cupboard. While there was no point in antagonising Luke further by deliberately going against his wishes, was there really any good reason why she shouldn't accept Rob's invitation? She owed Luke nothing—not even her consideration—after the way he had treated her. And, after all, Rob was *safe*; he didn't pull down any stars for her, he was simply pleasant company not to be taken too seriously. And Merrill certainly posed no threat to Rob's future with Heather, whatever Luke wanted to think.

'Oh, come on,' Rob persisted. 'I want to ask your advice about something. It's just an idea I've had and. . .' He stood up quickly as Luke appeared in the doorway.

'Idling again, Rob?' he said pleasantly, but his eyes flicked golden arrow-tips in Merrill's direction. '*You* might not be busy, but Merrill certainly is. Still, as you seem to have time to kill, how about looking over Delaneys' hardware catalogue?' He disappeared into his own office, and Rob came over to touch Merrill's shoulder hurriedly. Her mouth was set rebelliously, and she jumped under his touch.

'I sometimes wonder if Luke isn't jealous of me,' Rob whispered, grinning.

Merrill smiled crookedly. 'That might be funny if it weren't so utterly ludicrous.'

'One o'clock, then, in the wine bar.' Rob squeezed her shoulder, then joined Luke.

Jealous! That was a laugh, Merrill thought bitterly. She leaned back in her chair, raking long fingers through her hair and closing her eyes. Her job seemed to have carried her into ever deeper waters, for now she was very definitely embroiled in Luke's intention to see Rob safely married and out of danger of any possible distraction from the female staff.

Irritated, Merrill pushed her chair back. Surely Rob was old enough to manage his own affairs! So just who did Luke think he was, behaving like the father in some Victorian novel? Well, she decided emphatically, whatever *Luke* was, Rob was pleasant company, and surely what she chose to do in her own lunch-hour was entirely her own affair.

Even so, she had to admit to a sneaking sense of relief when Luke left the office just after twelve for a business luncheon; despite her defiance, she preferred that he didn't see her cross the road to the wine bar at one o'clock.

'Just soup, please, and coffee afterwards,' she ordered. 'Come on, then, Rob; you said you wanted some advice. And that,' she went on a trifle bitterly, the memory of the previous evening flooding back with renewed clarity, 'is the one thing that everyone enjoys giving.'

'Yes. Do you remember that I once spoke of holding an engagement party?' As Merrill nodded, Rob went on, 'Well, my mother will be home from her cruise on Saturday, and I've had this idea. . . I'll hold the party on Saturday evening. It'll be a nice welcome home for her.'

Merrill raised her eyebrows. 'So what advice do you want?'

'All in good time. About the party—I'd thought of making it a triple celebration: my engagement to Heather, Ma's homecoming, and a kind of—gesture of thanks to Luke.'

Merrill stared at him, her fingers absently crumbling a roll. 'What's Luke got to do with it?' she murmured.

For a moment Rob looked rather embarrassed. 'Oh,' he muttered, not looking at her, 'I suppose he's had—problems. With me, I mean. And he's always been pretty decent—bailing me out of rather tricky situations I got into, and not coming down too heavily about them.'

'I see.' Well, she supposed that figured; after all, she had seen Luke with the children at the sailing club, again revealing that other side of his nature which didn't extend to her. . . 'But I'm not sure that Saturday is a good day,' she continued. 'Luke has to go to York to see someone and——'

'That's the whole point, don't you see?' Rob said enthusiastically. 'We'll hold it at Luke's place, of course. My flat's too small anyway, and besides, Ma lives with Luke. It'll be a surprise for them both when they get home. . . Surprise parties are always the best. It can be arranged without his knowing a thing about it, and by the time he gets back it'll be in full swing.'

Merrill smiled, then after a moment said hesitantly, 'I don't know about your mother's reactions, of course, but are you sure it's the kind of surprise Luke will appreciate? If my information is correct, his meeting in York is likely to be rather sticky. In fact, I very much doubt that he'll come back in a party mood.'

'Oh, I think you're wrong,' Rob said emphatically. 'I know him better than you do. . . You only see the business side of him—that is, apart from last night,' he added with a meaningful smile. As Merrill's gaze dropped quickly, he hurried on, 'Oh, I'm not prying, although my intuition suggests that last night wasn't an unqualified success for either of you. . . But that's your affair.'

Absolutely, Merrill thought acidly. 'All right, then. You think Luke will enjoy a party. That leaves your mother. If she's coming back on Saturday, how are you going to keep it a surprise?'

'Oh, she won't be home until the evening. A friend's meeting her off the boat and driving her up.'

'So,' Merrill asked, putting down her spoon and sitting back, 'what advice can I give you? You seem to have it all worked out.'

'Well, it's more *help* that I need, really. . . I was wondering—Merrill, would *you* arrange things for me? You know—the food and so on. Of course, Heather could do it, but I want this to be a surprise all round. She loves surprises.' He smiled. 'If you could organise the catering and flowers and so on to be delivered to Four Winds during the late afternoon, say. . . What do you think of the idea?'

Rob was so obviously brimming with enthusiasm that Merrill had to say carefully, '*I* think it sounds delightful.' Still not entirely convinced about Luke's reaction, she added a cautionary, 'But will *they*?'

'Sure they will,' Rob said easily. 'So you *will* help?'

'All right,' Merrill said slowly, 'but on your own head be it.'

'And you'll come, of course?' Then, seeing her hesitation, he said, 'But you *must*! Heather wants to meet you. Besides, I'd like you to be there—especially as you'll have done all the work.'

Warmed by his tone, Merrill laughed. 'I think you could charm the birds out of their trees, as they say. . .'

she murmured. 'All right, then, I'll come—for a little while anyway.'

'Great.' Rob drew a sheet of folded paper from his pocket. 'I've jotted down a few details, numbers and so on. And some suggestions for food—something celebratory. And we'll have champagne, of course. Can I leave it to you?'

Merrill took the paper, glanced at it, then stood up. 'As Luke won't be back in the office until around three o'clock, and as the party's at such short notice, I'd better go and set the ball rolling.'

'I'm forever in your debt,' Rob said, striking a pose. 'We'll want waiters and waitresses, and everything cleared up afterwards. And money's no object; I want something really special.' He leaned forward to drop a light kiss on the end of Merrill's nose. 'And thanks again. You're a doll.'

It was fortunate that Luke didn't come in at *that* particular moment, Merrill mused later, as she reached for the telephone directory; he would certainly have misread Rob's little gesture of appreciation.

Before Luke arrived back she had arranged for details and menus to be sent to her home address, and she was humming softly when he came in. He shot her a suspicious glance which she met imperviously. She was quite looking forward to the party, after all. It would make a pleasant diversion in a rather low social life, and in the company of other people she would be able to give Luke a wide berth during the evening.

By Friday she had arranged everything to Rob's satisfaction, although as she handed Luke his notes for the meeting in York she still had some reservations about his reaction to his brother's methods of expressing gratitude.

* * *

Merrill was drying her hair on Saturday afternoon when Diane from the next flat knocked at the door and held out a letter addressed to Merrill, explaining that it had been included with her junk mail which she had ignored until a moment ago.

The handwriting was unfamiliar, and the letter had been addressed to Bracken Cottage and obviously redirected by Professor Wendell. Wondering, Merrill opened it slowly. Richard—Richard Stirling! Yes, of course, she recalled, he'd mentioned in Bruges that he would look her up when he was in the area. And naturally his only means of getting in touch would be to write to her at the one address he knew: Elise's cottage.

The letter was dated almost a week previously, and as Merrill read it she realised with dismay that Richard was already in the area and was suggesting that they meet in the lounge of Frobishers' at seven o'clock on Saturday—*this* evening.

I hope that you will have dinner with me, but if you can't make it, then telephone me at my London address before Thursday lunchtime, after which date I will be on my way up north and my movements are unpredictable.

'Damn,' Merrill said softly. Then, 'No, I didn't mean that. . .' Richard was a nice man, and ordinarily she would have quite looked forward to an evening with him. But it *would* happen tonight! She was surprised at the intensity of her disappointment at the prospect of missing Rob's party.

She sat down, running distracted fingers through her cool, damp hair. But perhaps she didn't have to miss it after all. On the very first occasion when an engagement party had been mentioned—that lunchtime when

Luke had joined Rob and herself—hadn't Rob suggested that she bring someone?

She stared thoughtfully at Richard's letter. Well, why not? One more person wouldn't make any difference to the arrangements, for Rob had thought it wise to cater for up to eight extra guests—'Just in case I'm more popular than I think I am,' he'd laughed.

No, there was absolutely no reason why she shouldn't take Richard along, and it might even be more comfortable to arrive with her own partner.

When she met him that evening and explained her predicament, he was happy to fall in with her plans. 'I feel like a bit of sociability after the enforced slog of research,' he said. 'We'll go in my car, and you can navigate.'

Rob looked quite different, dressed in a white dinner-jacket with a dark crimson bow-tie and matching cummerbund. 'Oh, my,' Merrill laughed, 'how splendid!'

'Didn't I tell you this was a very special occasion?' Rob twinkled. 'You're quite an eye-stopper yourself. . . Now come and meet Heather; she's in the dining-room having a last word with the catering people.'

'This is certainly some house he's got,' Richard remarked in a low whisper as they followed Rob along the hall.

'Oh, it isn't his house—it belongs to his half-brother, my employer,' Merrill explained hastily as Heather came forward, smiling.

'You've done a wonderful job,' she told Merrill after Rob had made the introductions. 'Everything's perfect. I didn't know a thing about it until Rob sprang it on me this afternoon.'

Merrill watched the petite figure, the vivacious face

with its generous mouth and dark, dancing eyes, and warmed to her immediately. 'Thank you, but it was Rob's idea. I merely set a few wheels in motion.'

'Rob's often spoken about you, and I'm so pleased you could come. I'll show you the cloakroom. . .' Heather turned to Richard. 'Come and get a drink—the room on your left. . .'

The few moments that Merrill spent in front of the mirror told her that she had made the right decision to wear the black dress which exposed one bare shoulder. Undecided, she had wondered if it might be too formal, but now she realised that this was going to be no jeans-and-sweater occasion.

She went back into the hall, then turned as the front door opened. For a moment she stared at a different Luke. He looked tired, a little subdued, and suddenly she was stunned by an almost overwhelming shock of tenderness. He looked like a man who needed a quiet evening, an easy chair, a drink, and soothing music unlike the vibrant strains of the rock number that reached them.

Then he saw her, at the same time his mind registering the music, and his eyes were guarded. 'Why, hello, Merrill,' he said, his voice dangerously soft. 'Is it too much to ask what you're doing here—in my house. . .?'

'I—that is, Rob. . . Rob wanted to hold a party here and ——'

'Did he indeed?' Luke frowned, his mouth hardening. 'I wondered what exactly was going on when I found I couldn't get into my own garage because of a great red car parked in the way.'

'Oh, heavens—that's my friend's car,' Merrill said hurriedly. 'I didn't think. . . I was so anxious to make sure that everything—that all the arrangements had been carried out satisfactorily that I——'

'"Curiouser and curiouser,"' Luke drawled. 'I take it that *you've* had a hand in this party, then?'

Merrill moved towards him, and as he dropped his briefcase on the chair with a weary gesture she said quickly, 'Please don't be cross. Let me explain. Rob wanted the party to be a surprise——'

'Then he won't be disappointed,' Luke said bluntly. 'I, for one, am *very* surprised.'

'He wanted to combine his engagement party with a party for his mother's homecoming and also to——'

'Do go on,' Luke murmured, watching her unblinkingly. 'You were saying?'

'He also wanted to—thank you for—for. . . Oh, *I* don't know,' Merrill mumbled. 'Ask him yourself. It's *his* party. All I know is that he thought you would be *pleasantly* surprised.'

Luke palmed his hair back with a gesture of resignation, and once again Merrill softened towards him. Instead of a quiet, relaxing evening which no doubt he had anticipated with pleasure, he was about to be confronted with a crowd of young people hell-bent on having a good time—and in his own home, too. For a moment she regretted that she hadn't tried harder to dissuade Rob from his plan. But it was too late now.

'Look,' she said quickly, 'why not let me get you a drink? And why not have a long, hot bath? Now, before too many people arrive. You'll feel a lot better.'

Surprisingly, he laughed. 'You mean—like *you* did, in Ghent, when Anna suggested it?'

'Well, it worked for me,' Merrill reminded him.

'It certainly did,' Luke said musingly. 'You became quite—— Oh, all right, then; it seems that tonight the choices aren't mine. I come home to find my half-brother has commandeered my house for his party, and now my assistant tells me to take a bath.' But the smile still eased the line of his mouth.

'Our motives are good,' Merrill said demurely, and turned away as he took off his coat. A few moments later she was putting a whisky tumbler into his hand.

'Thanks,' he said briefly, his eyes lingering on her face. 'You look like something extremely special.' His gaze moved to the velvety skin of her bare shoulder, and the tips of her nerves tingled their response.

'Do I?' she said breathlessly, trying to stem the little shivers. Then, lamely, she added, 'I had better ask my friend to move his car.'

'Oh, yes, your friend. . .' Luke said quietly, then turned abruptly into the inner hall which memory told her led to his bedroom. With a little sigh, a feeling of having come down to earth again, Merrill went to find Richard.

'Sorry,' she explained, 'but I was intercepted. Luke arrived, not too pleased about the party, and I tried to smooth him down. It's a surprise party, you see, and his first surprise was seeing your car blocking his garage.'

'Oh, Lord. . .that won't do anything for my popularity. I'll go and move it.'

The house began to fill up. Rob's friends were a lively, uninhibited crowd, and by the time Richard returned the party atmosphere was palpable, and Merrill had recovered from the disquiet provoked by her encounter with Luke. 'It's absolutely ages since I went to a party,' she remarked happily, as Richard handed her a tall, frosted glass.

'Well, as you had a hand in it it's only fair that you should enjoy it.' He grinned. 'One thing's sure—you won't be spending part of *this* evening mopping up in the kitchen!'

'I'm sure you're right,' she laughed, then glanced up to see Rob approaching with a tall, elegant blonde woman.

'Meet my mother,' he said.

'Stella,' she corrected. 'So you're Merrill. . . . Luke has often spoken of you. I think the word he used was *irreplaceable*, wasn't it, Rob?'

'Obviously an exaggeration,' Merrill demurred, thinking with a sudden sinking feeling, He's going to have to find a replacement soon. . .

'Don't be so modest,' Rob laughed. 'But surely it's time he was here. . .' He turned as Heather joined them.

Stella moved, and as the light caught her Merrill noticed that on the fine tanned skin there was an etching of small lines at the corners of her mouth and around her eyes, but she was still a very beautiful woman. Apparently Richard thought so, too, for after a moment he led her away to the bar.

'By the way, Rob,' Merrill said quietly, 'Luke *is* here, but he's tired and he's taking a bath. I met him in the hall——' she explained, and was going on to warn Rob to tone down his exuberance when she saw Luke coming towards them.

'Why, talk of the devil,' Rob interrupted, his slightly nervous tone making Merrill's warning superfluous, and betraying the fact that he wasn't as confident about Luke's reaction to the party as he had led Merrill to believe.

'From which,' Luke said smoothly, 'I must gather you're referring to me. I shall have words with you later, Rob,' he added significantly, then he turned as Heather slid her arm into his and stood on tiptoe to kiss his cheek. He gave her a brief hug. Then his gaze moved to Merrill as Heather pulled Rob away to meet a small group who had just come into the room.

After a brief, thick silence, Luke said smoothly, 'I see that you've brought your Belgian boyfriend along. I spotted him in the bar with Stella.' He paused for a moment, then went on softly, 'Lord, Merrill, but you must have made one hell of an impact in just one evening for him to come all this way, presumably simply to see you.'

Merrill stared at him innocently. Luke had jumped to the wrong conclusion about Richard, and she didn't intend to enlighten him—yet. It would be very refreshing to see Luke embarrassed, for a change. However, there *was* one small mystery. . . 'How is it that you recognised him?' she asked politely.

'Simply because I felt some responsibility for you in Bruges,' Luke replied evenly. 'I waited up just to make sure you got back to the hotel safely. After all, picking up strange men in strange towns. . . Anyway, sufficient to say that I witnessed the moment of your parting.'

'A casual, friendly kiss,' Merrill pointed out, but even so her face grew hot. 'I appreciate your concern, but I'm quite capable of looking after myself, you know.'

'Oh, I realise that *now*,' Luke said disparagingly. 'I wouldn't——' He broke off as Richard joined them.

'Oh, Richard,' Merrill said slowly, her eyes holding a glint of mischief, 'I'd like you to meet Luke Travis, my employer. Luke—Richard Stirling.'

'How do you do?' Richard held out his hand, and Merrill stood back a little, noting Luke's flash of surprise at Richard's West Country accent. But Luke recovered himself immediately. 'I believe you two met in Bruges,' he said neutrally.

Richard nodded. 'Quite a coincidence, wasn't it? Of course, we already knew each other slightly.' He stopped, his smile encompassing Rob and Heather who joined them then. 'Merrill and I had met previously— at a party in this area, actually.' He grinned. 'From now on I shall associate Nottinghamshire with good parties. It was at Merrill's cousin's place.' He looked at Luke. 'I wonder if you knew her—Elise Masters? An artist of some promise——?'

'She was one of our clients,' Luke cut in swiftly, and turned immediately to Heather, but not before Merrill had seen the shutter which had slammed down over his face at the mention of Elise. 'Ah, Heather,' he murmured, 'you found my package. . .?'

'I did.' Heather gave him an affectionate grin and held out a small white porcelain swan. 'The dear man knows that I collect swans,' she explained to Merrill and Richard, 'and he left it on the hall table with my name on a label around its neck. You know,' she confided, 'I sometimes think that one of the chief reasons why I'm marrying Rob is because it will get me Luke as a half-brother-in-law.'

'I don't believe a word of it,' Luke smiled. 'And now, how about introducing me to some of your friends seeing that they're enjoying the freedom of my house?'

After they had gone Richard said, 'Quite a guy. So that's the boss.'

'Very much so,' Merrill said shortly, still piqued by the curtness with which Luke had disposed of the subject of Elise. 'Let's find a seat, shall we?'

'Fine. I should have warned you that I don't dance, so I hope your evening won't be ruined.'

'Not at all.' Merrill's smile felt tight and false. Luke's dismissal of Elise as a mere client had rekindled all her misgivings. And yet Luke's presence, his magnetism, could so easily eclipse all her reservations about him. She was finding it increasingly difficult to sit here, in his home, trying to cope with the spectrum of emotions that chased pell-mell through her from one moment to the next, and at the same time evince a polite interest in Richard's remarks. She should have stayed away, had dinner alone with Richard somewhere, saving herself the pleasure and the pain of being near Luke. With a little start she realised that Richard was speaking.

'Truly, I don't mind not dancing,' she insisted. 'In fact, if you would prefer it, we can leave.'

Richard laughed. 'Stop being so unselfish. In a way, it's your party, too, so we'll stay and enjoy it. Now, let me bring you another drink.'

'Better make it a fruit juice this time, then,' she said. That was the safest drink when Luke was around.

When Richard had gone she sat watching the other guests; Stella was chatting animatedly to a lean, grey-haired man. Rob and Heather were the centre of a rather noisy young crowd. Then Luke materialised beside her, and with a shock of despair Merrill realised that, unconsciously, she had been watching for him.

He sat down, saying softly, 'I think you rather enjoyed that, didn't you?'

'I'm sorry?' She turned to face him, her eyes baffled.

'Oh, come on. . . You enjoyed my surprise on meeting Richard, of course,' he said. 'You had deliberately led me to believe that you'd picked up a stranger in Bruges, and naturally I had assumed him to be a Belgian.'

Merrill's eyebrows lifted. 'I can't see that his nationality is any concern of yours,' she answered.

'Now don't prevaricate,' he warned softly. 'You know what I mean.'

'And,' Merrill continued, 'if you jumped to the wrong conclusion in Bruges, that's your mistake. I simply didn't feel that it was important or necessary to enlighten you.'

Her voice was calm and matter-of-fact, but she had to fight the need to clench her hands in her lap. Luke's nearness seemed to reach into her core, sparking off those treacherous currents again, so that to even speak coherently at this moment was monumentally difficult. Consciously she relaxed her hands, at once willing Richard to return, yet hoping that he wouldn't—yet.

'Probably not,' Luke answered flatly, 'but I would have thought that your pride demanded that you correct my error.'

'Oh, *pride*. . . Anyway, it seemed pointless, considering that in your eyes I'm zero-rated anyway. Just as a matter of interest, would you have believed me if I'd said that I'd bumped into an old acquaintance near the museum?'

'Well, I might have,' Luke conceded thoughtfully.

'How magnanimous!' Merrill stared up, meeting his reflective sherry-coloured gaze. 'What am I supposed to do? Beg you to put aside your prejudice? Ask you to believe that I have morals, principles? That I'm not the kind of woman who deliberately exercises her feminine wiles on unsuspecting males? Like Rob, for instance?' she added fiercely.

'Calm down now,' he said, infuriatingly sensible. 'Can you blame me for holding the very opinion which you deliberately instigated? As for——' He stopped with a muttered oath as he saw Richard approaching.

'Actually,' he murmured, standing up, 'I was about to ask Merrill to dance. That is, of course, if you don't mind, Richard?'

'Not at all,' Richard smiled.

What else could she do, Merrill asked herself, but stand up, pleasantly acquiescent because of Richard's presence, and let Luke take her arm and lead her into a room which had been cleared for dancing? By a great effort of will she quelled the tremor that threatened as she went into his arms.

She held herself stiffly as the sensuous onslaught of his nearness battled with the frustration and bitterness that were never far from the surface whenever he was there.

'Why not relax?' he said softly against her hair. 'It's only a dance, you know.'

'What makes you think I'm not relaxed?' With the tempo of her heart quickening by the minute, her voice came uncertainly.

He leaned away from her a little, watching her face. 'I am fast learning to read you,' he began. 'And when I see that tilt of the chin, that lift of the head, I sense the mood.'

'How very astute of you, Luke,' she remarked.

'No, not astute, merely—aware.' He drew her closer to him again. 'All right,' he conceded, 'I may have been mistaken about Richard, but can you blame me? You—with all your chat about your full social life, your glamorous, eventful bachelor-girl programme, the get-up-and-go philosophy which you expounded so vividly the other evening in your flat? I was there, remember?'

'I don't think I'll ever forget,' she said numbly. That was an understatement: she was certain that she would *always* remember the feeling of being in his arms, the sensations his kisses and caresses had aroused in her— sad, beautiful ghosts which would haunt her forever. And then—revelation!—his motives laid bare.

'Nor I,' he said flatly. 'You made your point very

clearly. And yet——' his voice grew gentle '—a girl with eyes like smoke, a provocative nose, and a mouth designed for kissing——'

Desperately Merrill clung to the rags of her self-control. 'I think,' she said in a tiny voice, 'we disposed of that smooth-talking kind of approach on the evening under discussion, after I burned my thumb.'

'I see.' For a few moments they moved in silence, then he said, 'Just as a matter of interest, why did you come to this party?'

'Simply because Rob wanted me to meet Heather.' He surely didn't think that she was here because of *him*! She didn't even know if it was the truth. How could she, when her body had become a battleground for a crazy kind of chemistry?

'And do you like Heather?' Luke asked.

Merrill was relieved to change the subject. 'Oh, yes, I think she's delightful. She and Rob seem very happy with each other.'

'They are. So do me a favour, Merrill. Don't rock the boat.'

Merrill infused a note of boredom into her voice. 'I'm beginning to feel that I've been here before,' she murmured. 'That subject also was raised the other evening.'

'So it was, but I like to get things straight.' His cheek was against her hair, and in spite of all her reservations her body seemed to have grown limp and voluptuous. 'But,' he went on very quietly, 'you can rock *my* boat any time you like.'

'Really? Because you're—mature enough to cope with my get-up-and-go, self-interested philosophy?'

He nodded. '*I* think so.'

It was on the tip of Merrill's tongue to tell him how well he had 'coped' with Elise. She thought again of the diary, of the initial 'L' with a tiny laurel wreath drawn around it, of the intimate, secret hieroglyphics. But, again, Rob's party wasn't the right place to try to pin Luke down.

'In fact,' Luke was saying, 'now that you've got it into your head that Rob's happy with Heather, why don't we throw out all the aggro and start from scratch? We could even slip away now.'

Just for a moment Merrill allowed herself the luxury of imagination. With Luke's cheek against her hair, his arms a protective band, his thighs moving against her own, she was bathed in the potent sensuality of his closeness. And suddenly she wished that they were alone somewhere, just the two of them. Alone to explore the desires and passion which instinct promised her she had barely touched; alone to burn in the blaze that leapt between them. But longings were one thing; good judgement was another.

'No. No, we couldn't,' she whispered. 'This is Rob's party.'

'I'm sure he wouldn't mind.'

'But perhaps Richard would,' she insisted, a little wildly.

Luke's face darkened, then he said in a controlled voice, 'There's tomorrow?'

She gazed up at him. His eyes were intent, the golden gaze compelling, almost willing her to give him the answer he wanted; his features were uncompromising in their strength. Lucifer, she thought brokenly. . .Lucifer—the devil— temptation. . . 'No!' Then, more quietly, her voice steadying, 'I'll be busy tomorrow.' Thankfully, the music ended then and she was able to draw away from him. 'Well,' she said feebly, 'that seems to be that.'

'Yes. Thank you.' He nodded formally, a stranger

now. 'I mustn't keep you and Richard apart any longer. I'd better find Rob. If he's going to make a speech it ought to be before too much champagne goes to too many heads.'

He sketched a slight, mocking bow and left her, and Merrill went slowly along to the cloakroom. She felt as if she had been through a millrace, buffeted and whirled, but the one clear thought that ran through the inner tumult was the finally accepted fact that, with all her heart, she had wanted to say *yes* to Luke. To say it, and go on saying it.

Oh, what's the matter with you? her eyes asked her reflection as she retouched her lips, her boneless fingers taking forever to screw down the tube. She hardly recognised the vibrant image that looked back at her from the glass with wide, baffled eyes bright through weak, stupid tears.

The remainder of the evening passed in a vague haze of laughter and conversation until Rob's final kiss on Merrill's cheek as she and Richard left.

As he drove along the broad road leading back into the town Richard said idly, 'Are you in love with Luke, by any chance?'

'Good heavens!' Merrill's laugh sounded shrill in her own ears. 'What on earth makes you ask that?' Then she went on, more quietly, 'Of course I'm not! Confidentially I—I detest him.'

'Why work for him, then?' Richard asked reasonably.

'Because. . .' For a moment Merrill debated telling Richard the real reason. It might have been a relief to confide in someone, to get another person's opinion, especially as Richard had known Elise. But it was all too complex, too convoluted. 'Oh, because. . .well, naturally when I took the job I didn't realise that I would come to dislike him so much. That developed later. Anyway, I won't be staying much longer.'

When they reached her flat Richard accepted her offer of coffee, then left, and Merrill closed the door behind him thankful that the evening was over. One way and another, it had been an ordeal.

Then Richard was back. 'My car won't start,' he said disgustedly. 'May I phone for a taxi to the hotel? I want to leave by about ten tomorrow so I'll get on to a garage first thing in the morning and hope they can fix my car straight away.'

'What rotten luck. Yes, use my phone. Of course.' Then Merrill stopped. 'Why not use *my* car, though? It's late now, and it'll be quicker than waiting for a cab—and it's insured for all drivers. You can bring it back in the morning when you pick up your own.'

'Splendid!' Richard hugged her as she gave him the keys.

'It's the least I can do,' Merrill smiled, 'considering that you fell in so readily with my arrangements this evening.'

She walked with him to the garage, and as he got into her car she leaned forward and kissed his cheek lightly. Richard was the kind of man one *could* kiss, she thought later, as she kicked off her shoes. As with Rob, a kiss meant a gesture of friendship, nothing more. The other kind of kiss—the kind that Luke offered. . . She shivered. Still, wasn't that also unimportant, although in a less acceptable way?

However, there was also another difference, a dogged inner voice insisted: Luke's kisses left scars.

She reached up to remove her earrings, then noticed in the mirror that one was missing. Damn. They had belonged to her mother—silver and marcasite wings with a small pendant pearl; not valuable, but of personal importance.

Carefully Merrill took off her dress and shook it in case the earring was caught up somewhere in its folds. Then her face cleared; when she had leaned across to kiss Richard she must have nudged it off, and no doubt she would find it in her car when he brought it back in the morning.

CHAPTER EIGHT

MERRILL slept late on Sunday morning, and her first concern was for Richard. A quick glance through the window showed his car still parked outside, but by the time she had showered and breakfasted she saw that a mechanic was at work on it, and half an hour later her doorbell rang.

As she went to answer she noticed a white envelope addressed to her in Luke's handwriting lying on the doormat. She froze for a moment, then bent slowly to pick it up, her fingers confirming the shape of her earring inside.

She swallowed, a sickening vacuum opening up in her stomach. Her mind flipped back an hour—two hours? Her imagination visualised Luke—always an early riser—driving up to the house and immediately recognising Richard's car parked outside. And, knowing Luke, it was painfully obvious what conclusion he would have drawn, particularly in view of her remark last night that she would be 'busy' today. Naturally he would assume that Richard was staying with her for the weekend.

Richard—who was now standing at her door. . . She blinked, pulling her mind back to the present. She hoped that he wouldn't suggest coming up for a coffee; she didn't think she could rise to a social occasion at this particular moment, so she was thankful to accept her car keys, bid him a hurried, 'Safe journey,' and close the door again.

Fate, it seemed, had played right into Luke's hands,

confirming his suspicions about her with illuminating certainty and damning her as a liar. But there was nothing she could do about it, short of giving him an explanation for the presence of Richard's car outside her flat. And why should she make a production of it? Even if he cared, he probably wouldn't believe her anyway, she thought bitterly.

But brooding wouldn't help. With a steady breeze blowing, and a blue sky puffed with cotton-wool clouds, a day's windsurfing would concentrate her mind away from him, blow the shadows away, perhaps, and if by some chance Luke turned up at the club it would be easy enough to avoid him.

In the event he didn't, but as Merrill hung up her wetsuit in the garage upon her return her apprehension came back. He would have to be faced tomorrow.

As usual, he was at his desk before she arrived at the office, and, as always, she felt that brief but undeniable shock of pleasure at seeing him. It lasted only a few seconds, vivid enough to temporarily subdue any discord until their habitual attitudes towards each other slid into place again.

He didn't refer to the party, nor did he mention the earring, but the subject seemed to hang over Merrill like the sword of Damocles. She sensed that the barometer of their fraught relationship had plummeted to an all-time freeze and, at last, tormented beyond endurance, she stopped typing halfway through a schedule and went into his office.

He looked up, frowning coldly at her interruption. 'Yes?' he said stonily.

'I wanted to thank you for returning my earring. I didn't realise that I had lost it at the party.'

He brushed aside her thanks. 'It was no problem,'

he said. 'Someone picked it up, and Stella recognised it as yours.'

'All the same,' Merrill persisted doggedly, determined to get through to him, 'it was good of you to return it so promptly. They—the earrings—belonged to my mother, so I value them, and naturally I was very concerned when I realised that I had lost——'

'As I said,' Luke cut in, closing his desk diary with an impatient snap, 'it was no trouble. I had to come into town anyway; it was only a short detour to your place. And,' he went on, leaning back and watching her with a hooded gaze, 'considering the effort you put into Rob's party—which, incidentally, was voted a huge success—it was the very least I could do. And now,' he went on curtly, 'if we're not to continue discussing your family heirlooms, do you think you could spare a moment to run through some figures with me?'

Twin pink flags of annoyance unfurled in Merrill's cheeks. Did he have to be so deliberately rude?

'Because,' Luke went on, a frosted smile lengthening his lips, 'there's a lot to do today. I think the filing system needs streamlining. Can't think why you haven't done something to simplify Alison's methods.'

'I was saving it until I had time,' Merrill retorted, stung by this apparent criticism of her work.

'Well, that moment doesn't seem imminent,' Luke countered. 'In the meantime I suggest we cut down the cross-referencing. A progress chart, I'd thought, which would show at a glance——'

'I've made a chart,' Merrill said quickly. 'I worked it out during my second week here. Rather rough, I'm afraid, but I intended it only for my own use. However, it does give instant information and——'

'Well, well.' Luke's voice dropped to an answering

purr. 'Such anticipation! What *would* I do without you?'

The atmosphere in his office was like thin, cold glass. Suddenly the injustice of the whole situation, his expression, his attitude this morning, was the last straw. Merrill could take no more.

'Perhaps you'll soon find out!' She heard the echo of her words with a sense of incredulity. She had decided against announcing her intentions so soon. She prudently intended to wait at least until she found another job. But Luke's manner this morning was a series of whiplashes on painful flesh, and she'd had enough. She watched him with stormy eyes, the gold chain which she wore around her neck rising and falling with each agitated breath she drew.

His gaze had contracted to the merest topaz thread in a face where sudden bleakness polished his hard cheekbones to a dull, luminescent ivory.

No, she hadn't meant to tell him yet. But suddenly, on a great, surging crest of release, she was glad that she had! The end was in sight now, irrevocably; the end of a bitter, tormented, delirious part of her life. Soon it would be completely behind her, and she would be able to get on with living again, untroubled by the cataclysms of her emotions.

It must have been half a minute before Luke said in a scathing drawl, '*Find out*? You said I'll soon find out. Sounds ominous. . . what on earth does it mean?'

'Isn't it obvious?' Merrill flashed. 'It means, simply, that I intend to look for another job.'

Luke stood up suddenly, his body like a savagely coiled spring holding in check an inner core of violence. 'Would it be impertinent to ask why?' he gritted. 'Money, possibly?' His back was towards her as he crossed to the coffee-machine.

'No, it's not money.' Merrill was still possessed by a euphoric sense of freedom, and her tone was bemused.

'Then what?' he barked. 'You've made a success of your work, therefore I had assumed that you must enjoy it. Are you telling me now that you don't?'

'Work?' Merrill said vaguely. 'Oh, I love the work.' She was finding that it was easier to speak to his back than be forced to confront his frightening expression. 'Surely I don't have to spell out my reason for wanting to leave?'

'By all means *do* spell it out,' he retorted caustically.

'Oh, well, if you insist. . . The fact is that—that we're oil and water. Or hadn't you noticed? As I said, I love the *work*, but working with *you* is another matter. The truth is, I find it too—too stressful.'

'So that's it. Well, in that case, there's no more to be said. I'm sorry you can't stand the pace, Merrill, not to mention surprised. None of my previous assistants has ever suggested that I change my style of management, and I can assure you that I have no intention of starting now. No,' he went on weightily, 'not even in the interests of a firm which has always regarded continuity in its staff as of paramount importance to its operation.'

Merrill smiled wanly. 'That's quite a speech, and rather pompous, I thought. But perhaps I didn't make myself clear. Actually, I admire your—style of management, and I certainly wouldn't expect you to change it. What I'm trying to say is that when two people who neither like nor trust each other are thrust together, then something's got to give. Someone has to do something about it, and of course I'm the obvious person. So I'm doing it: leaving.'

'I see,' he said thoughtfully, waiting.

'Four weeks' notice is required, I believe,' Merrill

went on smoothly, 'so I should like it to take effect from today.'

'You——' Then, as if making a supreme effort to block out any fury from his voice, he said, 'Yes, that *is* a condition of employment, but I won't hold you to it. You may leave when you wish.'

'I'm prepared to fulfil the usual terms,' Merrill said steadily, 'and now, if we've exhausted the subject, maybe you have some ideas for improving the progress chart we spoke of. I'll bring it to you.'

'Leave it with me,' he said shortly when she laid the chart on the desk in front of him and stood back. 'Let's deal with the mail first, shall we?'

The letter bearing the Belgian stamp lay at the bottom of the morning's post. Merrill opened it, scanned it quickly, then passed it across to Luke, her heart sinking. It couldn't have been less welcome at that particular moment.

She watched Luke read it, saw the gathering frown carve two grooves over his aquiline nose. Then he looked up, a wry gleam in his eyes. 'Rather amusing, don't you think?' he said blandly. 'No, I can see from your expression that you are *not* amused. In fact, you're probably thinking that it couldn't have arrived at a less propitious moment.'

He dropped the letter on to his desk where it fluttered for a moment, an innocent reminder of the arrangement made in that grey stone house in Ghent. Then he rolled back his chair and stood up sharply as if needing to give vent to a violent sense of frustration. 'Of course, you *did* promise Anna that you would take her to Sherwood Forest the next time she and Sam came over on business,' he reminded Merrill tauntingly. 'Perhaps you shouldn't have been quite so generous with your offer.'

'I'll keep my promise, naturally. Anna's no problem,' Merrill observed airily.

'And,' Luke continued as if she hadn't spoken, 'it would be only common courtesy to return their hospitality to us and take them out somewhere to dine.'

'Of course,' Merrill agreed. 'But I don't see——'

'So,' Luke's voice overrode her own, 'I'm sure I needn't tell you that the evening has a better chance of success with four of us rather than three.'

'Come to the point, Luke,' Merrill snapped. 'Are you asking me to—to partner you for that evening?'

'Exactly,' he drawled. 'I knew that you'd get my drift. Of course,' he went on silkily, 'I'm aware that this might upset your arrangements with. . .now, what *was* his name?'

Merrill flushed suddenly. 'Richard,' she supplied. 'No, it won't upset any. . . As a matter of fact——' It was on the tip of her tongue to explain her relationship with Richard, but Luke cut in,

'Splendid. Then there's no problem. Just one thing, though.' He looked at her, his eyes glinting. 'Do you think you could possibly curb your dislike and mistrust of me for that one evening? Those were your words, I believe? We must make the best of an occasion which has overtaken us but which neither of us would want, given the choice.'

Merrill glared at him. He was enjoying this, she suspected. 'I'm sure you can find someone else to partner you,' she remarked stiffly.

'I'm sure I could,' he agreed, 'but why should I? Sam and Anna already know you, and as they both seemed to like you I'm asking *you*. The evening will be semi-business anyway, so your qualifications make you the best candidate.'

Defeated, Merrill stared down at the sheaf of letters

in her hand. 'All right,' she said at last. 'I see your point. And certainly after Sam and Anna's kindness to me I wouldn't want to seem ungracious.'

Luke let out a peal of genuine mirth, and Merrill stared at him stonily. 'Did I say something?'

'No, not really. Just put it down to my perverted sense of humour.' He took out his pocket diary and flicked through the pages. 'Book a table at the Tudor Queen for Saturday, will you, say eight o'clock? Sam and I can amuse ourselves on the Sunday, and that will give you the opportunity to take Anna to the Forest.' He closed the diary and put it away. 'Oh, you'd better telephone Sam at his office and let him have my suggestions.'

How easily he could dissemble, Merrill thought wearily as she drew up the chair and prepared to take his dictation. Despite her apparent composure, their exchange of words had left her feeling scalded, and she had to make an effort to concentrate on his quiet, clipped syllables. But business would always come first with Luke; she had always known that. A sudden deep misery welled up inside her so that her shorthand outlines blurred on the page. She blinked hard, blew her nose, and was relieved that Luke didn't appear to notice anything amiss.

When Rob put his head round her office door some time later, Luke had already left for an appointment. 'The coast's clear,' Rob whispered conspiratorially as he came into Merrill's room. 'Somehow I get the impression that Luke isn't too keen on my coming in here to chat to you, but I had to bring you these.' From behind his back he produced a sheaf of long-stemmed red carnations. 'For you,' he said, 'as a small token of my thanks.'

Although the flowers had no scent, Merrill buried

her face in their coolness to hide the tears which had
sprung again. What on earth was wrong with her? She
was turning into a real weepie! 'They're lovely, Rob,'
she murmured, moving away so that he shouldn't see
her weakness, and forcing herself to say, 'Luke told me
that the party was a huge success. I'm glad.' It was
difficult to believe that the party had been so recent;
too much had happened during the past thirty-six
hours.

'Hmm, I wouldn't have thought that Luke was in
any mood to judge,' Rob retorted, 'considering that he
was frosty-faced for most of the evening. Anyway, he
disappeared soon after you left—told Stella he'd had a
heavy day and was off to bed with a book. But it
certainly was a great party; you should have stayed
longer.'

'I was—rather tired. . .' Merrill turned to face him,
laying down the flowers on her desk. 'Rob. . .I've
decided to leave Woodline. You might as well hear it
straight from the horse's mouth.'

Rob whistled. 'Luke's not going to like that one bit,'
he said slowly, his blue eyes puzzled.

'Oh, he already knows. I told him this morning.'

'I'll bet he blew a gasket! Well, I'm very sorry,
Merrill. I'd say you're a real asset to the old firm, not
to mention highly decorative. So you've found a better
job?'

Merrill shook her head. 'I haven't even tried to find
another place yet.'

'A bit reckless, isn't it? I mean, you don't know how
long it'll be before you get something suitable. . . I had
an uncle like you,' Rob went on thoughtfully. 'Up and
away to greener pastures all the time. . .'

'Oh, it's nothing like that. Rob, you must have

noticed—Luke and I simply don't get along together, and there's a limit to how much friction one can stand.'

Rob grimaced. 'Oh, I know he's a bit single-minded about Woodline. . . He keeps his nose to the grindstone and thinks everyone else should. But that's probably because the firm was in a hell of a mess when he took over. Our father was a good designer, but he had no business sense.'

As Merrill raised surprised eyebrows, Rob went on, 'Didn't Luke tell you that? But no, I suppose he would have considered it disloyal to the old man. At heart, Luke's a good guy, really, and——' Then he stopped, frowning. 'I thought that. . .I mean, he took you out to dinner one night. Surely he wouldn't do that if you were both daggers drawn.'

'Oh, *that* evening. . .' Merrill dismissed it with a shrug, quelling the memory of Luke's kisses, the pleasant meal they had had. That, too, seemed like ancient history now. How perfect it all had been—until later. Her voice hardened. 'Luke had his reasons for taking me out, and I can assure you, Rob, that they had nothing to do with—with his liking me.'

'We-ll. . .' Clearly Rob was nonplussed. 'If you want to go, then—— But don't be like my uncle. He came to a bad end.' He grinned. 'Still, you'll come to my wedding, won't you? Some time in September, but Heather and I haven't fixed the date yet.' He held out his hand. 'Come? It's a promise?'

'A promise,' Merrill confirmed, grateful for the friendly strength of his warm hand. And September was a long time away.

During the following days Luke's energy for work seemed boundless, and it took all of Merrill's concentration to keep abreast of him. He seemed to be

possessed of a driving need to review and revitalise
everything, calling for frequent staff meetings, inviting
ideas on production methods and working schedules,
and when he wasn't at his desk or out at a meeting he
was cooped up with Mike Freeman in the downstairs
office or in one of the other departments.

His overcrowded programme allowed no time for
more than the barest formalities between himself and
Merrill, and his manner was coolly polite—a situation
for which, she told herself, she was profoundly grateful.

One morning when she was in his office working on
his personal files Mike came in for a discussion. At
first, Merrill paid scant attention to their conversation,
but her interest was caught when he and Luke began
speaking of environmental issues, rain forests, renew-
able sources of timber, and the possibility of turning
over a greater part of their production to make more
use of softwood.

There was no doubting Luke's dedication to the
subject, and against her will Merrill was impressed by
his fervour. The more she heard, the greater became
her respect for his views, and the lower her spirits
sank. Here was a man she could look up to, a man she
should like immensely—if she didn't have so many
reasons to dislike him! Oh, it simply didn't make any
kind of sense!

After a while Mike stood up. 'I hear you're leaving
us, Merrill,' he said, his eyes kind behind the heavy
horn-rims. 'Pity. I thought we'd got a good team. We'll
miss you.'

Merrill murmured her thanks, and then she was
alone in the office with Luke.

'Change your mind,' he said suddenly. 'Be part of
Woodline's great new venture.' His eyes were alight,
almost visionary, his face alive with a zeal that

smoothed out the harsh lines of the past days, and he was smiling.

As if in response, Merrill's own face seemed to come alive, and she felt her mouth answer that smile. As she passed him to put away the files she hesitated for a moment, and instantly his hand shot out to take hers in a crushing grip. 'I meant it,' he said quietly. 'Don't leave.'

Shaken to her depths by his touch, Merrill wavered for a moment. Then gently she withdrew her hand. 'I must.'

'Just because of a stupid argument that had nothing whatever to do with your job here?'

'N-no, not only that——'

'Why, then? There's another reason?' When she nodded, he said, 'Then why not tell me?'

Merrill sighed. 'Maybe I will, but not now.' The atmosphere in his office seemed to be closing in on her in an intimacy which she must avoid at all costs. 'Besides, as I've already told you, it—you and I together—it doesn't work. Or,' she amended, 'it might work sometimes, in snatches, but——'

The old familiar shutters came down over his gaze. 'Stupid of me,' he said, palming back the white strand in his hair. 'Of course it wouldn't work when one of us is determined that it shouldn't. I'd forgotten—got carried away.' He smiled crookedly. 'Felt like a crusader. How juvenile. Now,' he went on briskly, 'you've sorted out the files? And you've cleared that query with Maslins'? Good, because with this new project in the offing I'm going to be working to a very tight schedule. And so are you.' He paused for a moment. 'And as you insist on leaving at the end of the month,' he added blandly, 'I'd like everything—but *every-thing*—bang up to date.'

'But of course,' Merrill said airily. 'Everything will be. You're entitled to your pound of flesh.'

He nodded. 'Yes. That's just what *I* figured.'

With the weekend approaching Merrill felt a deepening of her apprehension. Naturally she was looking forward to seeing Anna again, and it would be pleasant to have her company on Sunday. However, there was Saturday evening to get through first. And there lay the crux of her unease; she couldn't be absolutely sure that it wouldn't present some emotional problem. The trouble was *Luke*; the trouble had always been Luke.

After all the hassle they should know exactly where they stood with each other, Merrill thought as she dressed on Saturday evening. Yet an evening with Luke was totally unpredictable. If only he were boring, or humourless, or just plain unattractive. . . But he was too—too exciting, dynamic. He had too much power to uplift and knock down.

Oh, blast! she thought, smudging her eyeshadow and hunting for a cotton-bud. Why didn't I tell him that I had an absolutely unbreakable date? Still, she could console herself with the knowledge that Luke, and all his complexities, wouldn't be impinging upon her life for much longer. And when she showed him Elise's diary he would collapse like a house built of cards. She stopped suddenly, her hand frozen in mid-air. It was almost impossible to imagine Luke defeated and flattened.

You're getting dithery, my lass, she told herself; dithery and nervous. . .

The doorbell rang twice, sharply, interrupting the vacillation of her thoughts. She reached for her handbag, and with a hurried final glance at the mirror to reassure herself that none of the inner turmoil showed she locked the flat and went out.

'You look and smell quite delicious,' Luke remarked with detachment. 'And I don't need to tell you that I'd appreciate your whole-hearted co-operation this evening. I'm hoping to do a lot of business with Sam when we get this new programme off the ground.'

'Aren't you rather overstating my role in all this?' Merrill asked, fastening her seatbelt and wishing that he weren't so devastatingly attractive. His dark suit was impeccable, his hair was exactly the right length, and the fragrance of his aftershave was just sufficiently elusive as to be almost unbearably tantalising.

'Not at all. Oiling the wheels, smoothing the path— very necessary components which pay dividends. Well? Is it a deal?' He turned to look at her as he put the car into gear, and the glint in his eyes rekindled the unwelcome wildfire in her veins.

She nodded, stifling a sigh at her own vulnerability.

Luke was silent as he drove. Sunset was still a couple of hours away, but the town roofs seemed touched with a silver gleam. As they waited at a pedestrian crossing Merrill watched a boy and girl kiss by the fountain in the square, then she blushed as she realised that Luke was watching her. He began to speak of Stella's interesting experiences during her cruise, of the cookery course that Heather had enrolled for, and of Rob's house-hunting forays.

Merrill sensed that he was trying to put her at her ease, building a bridge over the rift that divided them, to get the evening off to a good start. As always, his knack of disarming was successful, and she was even laughing as they went into the foyer of the Tudor Queen where Sam and Anna awaited them.

From the beginning, the evening bore all the hallmarks of success, Luke adapting himself immediately to the light holiday mood of Sam and Anna, and sweeping Merrill along with him. After a few moments she had relaxed fully, her apprehension shrivelled by the atmosphere of friendliness and laughter.

As she sipped an aperitif it dawned on her that this would be the last social occasion which she and Luke would share, so why not just tread water?

She glanced up to see Luke's gaze fixed upon her, warmly approving. He gave a barely perceptible nod as if he had read her mind and applauded her attitude. She smiled back and, for some reason, blushed again. But it wasn't that fierce, unpleasant upsurge of heat; this was quite different—a warmth, a harmony, an acknowledgement that at times they could be in perfect accord.

'Now who says you have to go to the Continent for a superb meal?' Sam asked contentedly as, later, they moved towards the coffee lounge.

'Was it *only* the meal, Sam?' Merrill widened her eyes in feigned disappointment. 'Didn't the *company* help at all?'

'Oh, undoubtedly.' Sam laughed, his gaze lingering on her animated face. 'In fact, I've half a mind to join you two girls tomorrow in Sherwood Forest, and perhaps we could arrange to lose Anna somewhere in the bosky glades.'

'Not a chance,' Luke said easily, grinning. 'Tonight is the sweetener; tomorrow you and I talk business.'

'And besides,' Anna put in, 'considering that Sam's idea of exercise is moving from one chair to another, he probably wouldn't even *make* the bosky glades!'

It was clear that Anna had no worries about her husband's attempts to flirt; it must be wonderful,

Merrill reflected, stirring her coffee, to have that kind of trust, that complete security in love.

'This is one of the best evenings I've had in a long time,' Sam said, sipping his coffee. 'You and Luke go well together.'

'Like a music-hall act?' Luke laughed, then said to Anna, 'When you've done Sherwood Forest, why not take a look at Newstead Abbey? You know—Byron's place.'

'"Mad, bad, and dangerous to know,"' Merrill quoted softly. She looked up and caught Luke's glance, a sudden question in his eyes. A tingle rippled through her blood. He wasn't in the least like Lord Byron physically, yet perhaps the epithet wasn't completely irrelevant.

'I've got a better idea,' Sam said, leaning forward. 'We'll *all* go to Newstead. The girls can walk their legs off in Sherwood Forest while you and I, Luke, get down to business, then we'll join them later.'

For a moment Merrill thought that Luke was going to turn down the idea, but Sam persisted, 'After all, there's no harm in combining business with sightseeing, is there?'

'None whatsoever,' Luke said equably. 'Is that all right with you, Merrill?'

After only a momentary hesitation she nodded. Circumstances seemed to be conspiring to throw them together. But at least she wouldn't be alone with him. Those were the dangerous moments. She shivered suddenly.

He noticed. 'Sit here,' he said quickly, getting up to change seats. 'You'll be nearer to the radiator.'

Merrill smiled wanly. What difference could a radiator make to an inner, more profound temperature?

CHAPTER NINE

'So *THIS* is Sherwood Forest!' Anna's voice sank to a note of disappointment as she read the roadside sign with its oak-leaf logo. She stared out of the car window where the wheat fields, blue-green in the sunshine, undulated towards the distant headstocks of a colliery.

Merrill laughed at her dejection. 'Don't worry. . .this whole area was once part of a vast forest. Over the centuries clearings were made and settled. I promise that when we park the car you won't be disappointed. There's more than enough actual forest left for you and me.'

'I'm glad to hear it. I don't like having my illusions shattered.'

'Perhaps it's better not to have any in the first place,' Merrill remarked idly, braking at a crossroads.

'Oh, but wouldn't life be dull? We need illusions; they don't *always* get shattered, and reality sometimes actually surpasses them.'

'If you're lucky,' Merrill murmured.

'Don't sound so cynical. . . I shall want to get some souvenirs to take home, by the way.'

'That's no problem; there's a shop, also a village close by. Just sit back and enjoy it.'

Later, as they were making their way through the bracken, Anna said casually, 'Sam told me that you're leaving your job with Luke.'

'Yes.' In an attempt to soften her abruptness, Merrill stopped to point. 'Do look at that dead tree,' she remarked. 'Doesn't it remind you of a Disney film?'

144

Anna stopped and swung up her camera, angling it towards the shattered trunk and the grotesquely tortured boughs. 'I can just imagine,' she murmured, 'that when midnight strikes it will come to life and walk or dance on those twisted roots. And look—you can almost see a face in the lumps and fissures of the bark.' She clipped the cap over her camera lens and joined Merrill again. 'I've been wondering—of course, it's none of my business—but why are you leaving Woodline?'

Merrill stifled a sigh. So her attempt to deflect this topic of conversation had failed. 'I think I should like a change,' she said slowly after a moment.

Anna nodded. 'I suppose Luke might be a difficult man to work for,' she ventured.

'No. Yes. That is—in some ways,' Merrill said lamely.

'Ah.' Anna stopped to examine the great plates of fungus growing out from a tree-stump. 'I expect you prefer someone like that man in London you told us about—the one with all the medicines.' She paused by a silver birch sapling, looking at Merrill quizzically. 'Someone dull, steady—safe?'

'Perhaps,' Merrill conceded. She looked away from Anna's enquiring face, fastening her gaze on the spread of old bracken through which this year's green shoots thrust. Anna's blue eyes seemed to see too much, and Merrill had already had enough of that discomfiting shrewdness from Luke. 'Look, if we turn along this path we come to the most celebrated tree in the forest—the Major Oak. And you *must* get a photograph of *that*. Everyone does. Then how about some lunch? There used to be another tree, I believe, known as Robin Hood's Larder. . . And while we eat I'll entertain you with tales of Robin. There are stories that he was a friend of the Plantagenet kings—you know, Richard *Coeur de Lion*, and John who lost the Crown Jewels. . . Of course, parts of Yorkshire claim Robin for their own. . .' With a small detached part of her mind she heard her quick, breathless words and realised that she was chattering. Another part of her mind was still registering the fact that, at some time during last evening, Luke must have mentioned her impending departure to Sam who, presumably, had told Anna.

It was just as likely, therefore, that any revelation to Anna—by word or expression—might be relayed to Sam and, perhaps unintentionally, onward to Luke. And Merrill didn't want to think of Luke and that hollow, unsatisfied feeling that had followed when she'd seen him drive away last night. In fact, today's activities had offered some hours of reprieve from thoughts of him—at least until such time as they were due to meet up later in the afternoon. She hoped that Anna would keep off the subject of Luke for the next few hours.

But she need not have worried. Tales of Robin Hood were very much to Anna's romantic taste, and she listened enthralled as Merrill searched her memory for the legends and folklore she had grown up with. Anna's energy, too, proved inexhaustible; she was determined to see as much as they could possibly crowd in—even the little church where Robin was reputed to have married Maid Marian.

'And now,' she said much later, as they got back into the car, 'for Lord Byron. I wonder if he really *was* mad, bad and——'

'Dangerous to know?' Merrill grinned. 'It would seem so. But he had his good side, too.'

On the mile-long drive up to the Abbey Anna

exclaimed with admiration at the banks of rhododendrons in bloom at each side of the narrow road, and they were chatting with the familiarity of old friends as Merrill pulled into the car park.

With a fluttering return of nervousness she recognised Luke's car immediately. He and Sam were sitting inside, talking as they waited, and judging by Luke's expression his day had gone well.

Dutifully she and Luke followed Anna and Sam through the house; they discovered that they had both visited it several times in the past. 'We might as well not be here,' Luke murmured, as their guests constantly referred to the information sheets and argued amicably about the exhibited memorabilia.

'It's all in the interests of good business relationships,' Merrill said sweetly. 'And it was your idea, you know.'

He gave her a sidelong glance. 'So it was,' he said idly. Then, 'Enjoy your walk?'

'Oh, very much. It was more than a mere walk. . .I think Anna's an exercise freak,' Merrill laughed. 'Unlike Sam.' She eyed his stolid figure indulgently. 'He's a nice man, though.'

'As was obvious last night, he likes you, too,' Luke returned.

Merrill turned away. Surely he wasn't implying that she had been trying out her feminine wiles on Sam? She wouldn't put it past him. Her barbed comment died unspoken as Anna straightened up from a glass cabinet. 'Strange, and rather nice, that a dog's collar should still be here after almost two hundred years,' she said softly.

'Oh, Byron loved Boatswain,' Luke told her. 'There's a memorial to the dog in the grounds. You'll find the inscription rather moving, too.'

'So you see, Anna—he couldn't have been *all* bad,' Merrill reminded her.

'Few people are. Or perhaps you hadn't noticed?' Luke put in softly, his quirked eyebrows lending a deeper, more personal value to the words, and Merrill found the opportunity to murmur,

'You surprise me. I didn't think you had that much tolerance and imagination in you.'

His mouth tightened. 'Ah, but then you don't know me. Do you?'

Enough, Merrill thought; I know you well enough.

Outside again, Anna stared over the sweep of lawns. 'A waterfall!' she exclaimed. 'I must take another photograph. And one of that peacock. Then we'll walk through the trees. Come on, Sam, you've lounged about enough today.'

Merrill concealed a smile as Sam groaned, but Anna was already striding ahead, her camera trained on the peacock which chose that moment to display.

The path through the beeches was narrow, and Merrill, against her will, found herself walking with Luke as Sam staunchly strode ahead, matching his wife's energetic pace.

'By the way,' Luke began, 'thanks. I'm about to clinch a very attractive deal with Sam's firm, and all this——' he gestured '—has helped. Obviously Anna has enjoyed the weekend, and that's largely due to your efforts.'

'It's been my pleasure,' Merrill said airily. 'And, besides, a personal assistant's tasks are legion. As a matter of fact, *I've* enjoyed the day very much indeed, so you don't have to make a big thing of being grateful.'

'I wasn't aware that I *was* making a—big thing,' Luke said acidly. 'So there's no need to be so prickly. . .'

'Now isn't that strange?' she countered. 'That's exactly the term I would use to describe *you*!'

'Waspish as ever! Can't you give yourself a day off?' Luke growled.

'That's what I'm trying to do, right now! Do please let me indulge myself. . .' Merrill slowed, staring up at the expanse of blue sky trapped between the great grey beech branches. 'It's rather like a cathedral,' she murmured. 'The tree are the pillars, and the path the aisle and——' She stumbled suddenly, one knee crumpling.

Instantly Luke's hand was beneath her elbow, supporting her. With a stab of pain that went far deeper than mere physical agony Merrill felt the electric charge of his touch surge through her. 'Thank you, but I'm—I'm all right,' she whispered shakily.

'Are you?' Luke's eyes stared down into hers, his gaze drawing up a veil of heat in her body until she was suffused by a sensation that blocked out everything but his closeness. Only the grip of his hand on her arm joined their bodies together, yet the union seemed complete and total so that she was no longer a separate entity. Sam and Anna had disappeared round a curve in the path. They might not have existed. There was no one in this world but herself and Luke, wrapped in a profound, pulsating silence.

His head bent quickly as his other arm drew her against him. Merrill knew what was coming and hadn't the strength to resist. With a stifled groan that for some reason moved her deeply, his lips found hers with a sweet fire that seemed to sear her very soul. Passion and tenderness mingled as his mouth moaned against hers, drowning her tiny exclamation of despairing acceptance. His arms tightened as if he would absorb her completely, grinding her into himself in a desperate assuagement of an age-old hunger.

She turned her head suddenly, and his lips blazed a path to her ear. 'No,' she whispered brokenly. 'Oh, please. . .no. . . Can't you see——'

'You talk too much,' he said roughly. 'You're always arguing, always saying *no*.' His lips were teasing her lobe unbearably, bringing all her senses to a crescendo of awareness. 'Always pushing me away,' he went on, his words muffled against her skin. 'Your eyes and your lips tell me one thing; your mind, your voice, your hands *protest*. . . What are you trying to do to me, Merrill? And *why*, for heaven's sake? Why?'

Merrill shook her head blindly. How on earth could she even begin to answer that question? But she couldn't, *mustn't* let him kiss her again. Couldn't he see what he was doing to *her*? And was this how he had got under Elise's skin?

And, as always, the thought of Elise lent her a much needed strength. She whipped out of his arms. 'I—I don't know what you're talking about,' she whispered after a moment.

'Oh, yes, you do.' He was gazing at her unblinkingly, his eyes darkened by desire, but she sensed that the old anger was surfacing again. 'You know very well what I'm trying to—— Ah, *hell*.'

He stepped back suddenly, then took Merrill's arm, propelling her forward towards Sam and Anna rounding the bend in the path.

'We had to turn back,' Anna said gaily. 'The path led nowhere.'

Merrill kept her face averted as they walked back towards the Abbey. She didn't want Anna to see her confusion and jump to conclusions which, in this case, would be the right ones. Still trying to pull herself together, Merrill chewed her inner lip crossly. Damn Luke. He didn't miss an opportunity. Well, he wouldn't, would he? she argued fiercely with herself; he thought he knew the type of girl she was. And on most of the occasions when they had been alone together he hadn't let a chance slip by. She wasn't safe from him. But, more importantly, she wasn't safe from herself, from the needs which his merest touch evoked. And, judging from what he'd said today about—about eyes and lips, she hadn't managed to conceal those needs.

As they skirted the smooth lawns on the way back to the car park Merrill dropped behind to walk with Sam who was now complacently asserting that all this exercise had given him an appetite for dinner. 'And you'll join us of course, Merrill?' he concluded.

'Well, I——' Merrill paused uncomfortably. The last thing she wanted was to prolong the agony.

Luke turned sharply. Obviously he had overheard, but before he could speak Merrill said hurriedly, 'I—I'm sorry, Sam, but I can't. I already have a date this evening.'

'Then break it, my dear,' he said sweepingly as they reached Luke's car.

'Oh, come, Sam,' Luke put in, jingling his car keys and eyeing Merrill narrowly, 'that's hardly fair. You can't expect Merrill to alter her arrangements at a moment's notice. It might be a very important date.' His tone was pleasantly idle, but there was a twist to his mouth which didn't escape Merrill.

'Oh, all right,' Sam grumbled, 'but it's a pity, especially as Anna and I leave tomorrow. Still, I guess we've encroached enough on your weekend, and a girl like you is bound to be in demand,' he twinkled.

'And that,' Luke breathed, 'is probably an understatement.' More audibly, as he opened the car door for Anna, he went on, 'Sam, why don't you and Anna come back to my place? Stella's away, but I can rustle up something simple.'

'That sounds very relaxing,' Anna smiled.

'So,' Luke said, turning to Merrill, 'Sam and Anna will be going back with me.' He nodded as if in dismissal, and Merrill guessed that he was still angry with her. 'I'll see you in the office tomorrow.'

Briefly, but with an acute sense of utter aloneness, Merrill said her goodbyes to Sam and Anna and went over to her own car.

Along the drive to the Abbey gates she was aware of Luke's car reflected in her rear-view mirror. Then, when they turned out on to the main road, Luke overtook her with an authoritative toot. As she watched them disappear into the distance she shivered with the chill of her own isolation.

'Feeling tired?' Rob's voice broke through Merrill's lethargy the following morning. She looked up from the minutes she was collating.

'Not particularly,' she defended. 'Why?' She waited warily. If he was leading up some further project which required her co-operation, the answer would be no. She had no intention of putting herself deeper into Luke's bad books; all she wanted now was for her involvement with Woodline Design to proceed peacefully to its end. It was the only way out for her.

'Oh, nothing,' Rob said. 'It's just that Luke invited Heather and me to join him and his friends for dinner last night. They mentioned that you and Anna walked a hundred miles and that you were following it up with a heavy date. Sam was bereft by your absence,' Rob teased.

'Oh, yes, I'm sure he was,' Merrill murmured saltily. 'Well, if that's all you came to tell me, then you won't mind my pointing out that I *am* rather busy. . .'

'Getting everything up to date before you depart? I can't think why you're going,' Rob grumbled. 'This place won't seem the same. No, I really came to see if you've got any tweezers. I was down in the workshops and I've run a great splinter into my thumb.' He held out his hand for Merrill's inspection.

She reached for her handbag. 'You're in luck. Better come over to the window.' She made a sympathetic noise. 'It's a big one. . . Now hold steady; I don't want to break it.' She bent over Rob's hand and slowly, deftly drew out the sliver of wood. 'There,' she said playfully as he winced, 'all done now. It wasn't too painful, was it?'

'You're so kind,' he quipped softly. 'Efficient, obliging, beautiful, and with the touch of an angel.'

Merrill dropped the tweezers and laughed. She was certainly going to miss Rob. 'And you bring a little sunshine into my life, too,' she grinned. 'But what would *you* know about angels' touches—a self-confessed young sinner like yourself?'

'Has someone been spreading malicious gossip?' he asked innocently, and reached for her hand.

Merrill laughed again, then glanced up, the laughter dying in her throat at the sight of Luke leaning nonchalantly in the doorway of his office, the expression of locked-in fury contradicting his easy stance.

'Rob,' he said very quietly, 'where the hell have you been? I've rung around the place for you. I should like you to drive out to see Maslin immediately. There's a hitch with those fittings they're supplying.' He jerked his head. 'So come through, will you, and I'll spell out the details?'

For a few minutes Merrill heard the murmur of their voices, followed by the sound of Luke's outer door closing. A moment later he appeared in her office. He walked up to her desk and stood looking down at her. 'I'm going to speak very plainly,' he said in that same quiet and rather alarming tone. 'In spite of all I've said, all I've *asked*, the message doesn't seem to have got through to you yet.'

'Oh, *really*,' Merrill said wearily, 'you're not *still* accusing me of trying to lure Rob away from Heather?'

'I don't know *what* your motives are,' Luke snapped suddenly, 'but your methods look——'

'If you must know,' Merrill interrupted stonily, 'I removed a splinter from Rob's thumb. You don't believe me?'

'Rob knows where the first-aid box is,' Luke retorted, 'and it's not in *this* office! You'll have to do better than that.'

Merrill glared at him, her temper rising. 'If you don't believe me, ask Rob. If he chose to come to me, then that's his——'

'And I'll tell you why he came to you, shall I?' Luke's eyes glinted dangerously. 'Because he knows that he's always welcome here, that you'll flirt with him, play him along and——'

Merrill stood up suddenly, her fists clenched against her sides, her eyes a glacial blue-grey. 'I give Rob as good as I get,' she whispered. 'And that's *all*! It's simply the—the conversational currency between us. It means nothing—to either of us. Good gracious,' she breathed, 'if you really do believe that Rob and I are conducting some sultry little affair, do you think that either of us would be fool enough to use an office which adjoins yours?'

An idea rocketed into her mind, and without stopping to examine it she rushed on, 'Is it possible that you even thought that *Rob* was my date last night? Well, is it? And is that why you invited him and Heather to join you in the evening? Tell me, Luke,' she went on, watching him intently, 'were you keeping tabs? Checking up?'

Luke's eyebrows drew together in a thunderous bar. 'Oh, for heaven's sake,' he growled, 'of course not. I simply——'

'Well, I wouldn't put it past you! You're paranoid about Rob and me,' she said furiously.

'Maybe I believe I have some reason to be.' His eyes were yellow ice, and a little pulse flickered in his hardened jaw. 'Perhaps that kind of thing runs in families—in the blood.' There was an ominous undertone in his words which wasn't lost on Merrill.

'What exactly are you trying to say?' She met his gaze levelly.

'Only that—that your cousin also had this *femme fatale* approach,' he bit out.

For a moment Merrill's eyes widened uncomprehendingly. Then, with a sickening thud in her solar plexus, she understood. Elise! He was referring to Elise! How *dared* he speak of her dead cousin in that scathing voice? And, after all those earlier occasions when he had carefully skirted round the subject of Elise, was this, at long last, a confession of his involvement?

In an instant Merrill's anger had consumed itself by its own intensity. She felt burnt out, an empty shell. Let him have the final word. She was too drained to carry on this impossible, futile war any longer.

She turned away. 'Well,' she said defeatedly, 'I suppose *you* should know.' Unseeing, she opened a

cupboard and leaned weakly against the shelves, waiting for him to go, willing him to leave her alone.

For a moment Luke still stood there as if he intended
to say more, but Merrill couldn't bring herself to look
at him. The atmosphere of enmity seemed like an ugly
noise in her pleasant office. There were no half-
measures with Luke, she thought, strangling a sob; he
was a man of passion, whether in anger or in—in. . .
She pressed her lips together, welcoming the pain of
her teeth biting into their softness. After a moment she
heard Luke leave, and the door of his office closed
behind him.

Blindly she moved back to her desk again, to the
neat pages she had been stacking when Rob had come
into the room. What an age ago that now seemed. She
put nerveless fingertips to her hot cheeks. Her eyes
stung with tears. She couldn't take any more. She
really couldn't. Luke was proving impossible to work
for.

Hastily she dashed the back of her hand over her
eyes, stapled the minutes together neatly and folded
them into their respective envelopes. That job was
complete. So, now was her own.

She reached for her jacket, knotted the gay red scarf
at her throat and tapped at Luke's door, then went in.

'Yes?' His face was an arrangement of harsh lines so
discouraging that she almost lost her nerve and backed
out.

But she forced herself to stand her ground; the
sooner this was over, the better. Moistening dry lips,
she began, 'You'll remember that when I told you I
intended leaving you said I might go immediately? You
remember?'

'I do,' he said curtly. 'Well?'

'I'd like to take you up on that offer.'

'I see.' A bleached patch appeared suddenly around his mouth, but his tone didn't change. 'Very well. I'll see that your salary is made up to this date and a cheque posted on to you.'

She swallowed. 'Thank you.' They were like strangers, she thought dumbly, foreigners from different worlds.

'But there's something else?' he asked, as she didn't move.

'Yes.' Merrill summoned up the remnants of her ebbing courage. 'When I first came here—to Woodline Design—it wasn't as you thought. I didn't come as an applicant for the job you'd advertised. I merely called to settle Elise's account. But you assumed I'd come in answer to your advertisement. So I went along with it.' She paused, then drew a shuddering breath. 'Working for you seemed to offer an opportunity to learn what kind—what kind of man you were—what kind of man my cousin was involved with so recently before her death.'

The harsh strength in his face didn't weaken, but she saw that he was listening with cold concentration to her words. She forced herself on. 'You see, I was never fully able to accept that Elise's death was due to a—to a road accident.' She swallowed again; her throat seemed constricted with tears. 'I mean. . .well, the *accident* could have been the result of—of a certain—state of mind.'

Luke regarded her with narrowed watchfulness. 'I'm listening,' he said, 'but what's all this supposed to mean? And what has it to do with me?'

Just for a fraction of a second Merrill felt that his surprise was genuine. Then she quashed the thought; naturally he would pretend to be surprised, to have no idea of what she was getting at.

'Oh, you know,' she said dully. 'You as good as admitted it a few moments ago, although *your* opinion of Elise doesn't coincide with mine. . . But in any event I've known all along that you were involved with Elise. You see, she left me everything. And it was necessary, purely for business reasons, for me to go through her diaries. I had to find out what commissions she had which would have to be cancelled. And I learned things about—about her private life. So there's no point in trying to bluff it out, Luke.'

Even at such a moment Merrill had to admire his talent for self-control. No flicker of guilt crossed his face, no softening. Instead, if anything, his features were knotted more tautly. For a moment she regretted that she had forfeited the supreme triumph of thrusting the diary entries in front of his face. But yet, once more, events had made a bonfire of her plans.

'So,' she went on, fighting to maintain a cold, level rhythm in her words, 'I came to Woodline to learn what kind of man you were, just as I said. And now I know. I learned something else, too. Apparently you weren't averse to trying to score with *me*—on the occasions when it suited you. And perhaps your arrogance tells you that *I* encouraged *you*—up to a point, that is—in the same way as I'm supposed to have encouraged Rob. But, just for the record, you're wrong on both counts.'

'And now you're going to tell me that you're not that kind of girl,' he said, his lips barely moving.

'Exactly. But I don't expect you to believe it. Nor do I care very much.' Something inside Merrill protested at the lie, but she went on stonily, 'I think I had your measure before I ever set foot in these offices. Oh, yes, Luke whatever you might *say*, I gathered quite a lot of hard facts from Elise's diaries.'

Luke got up quickly, sending his chair rolling back to hit the wall behind his desk with a crash that made Merrill jump. 'Now just listen——' he began.

But Merrill had backed away and was standing at the door. 'No,' she whispered. 'No, I will not listen. You have nothing to say which I want to hear. I'm going now. I'm quite sure some agency will oblige you temporarily until you can find another assistant. There's some post on my desk—those minutes. . .' She turned quickly, ran through her own office and down the stairs.

Once outside, she stood uncertainly for a moment, oblivious to the curious glances of passers-by. Then instinctively she looked back at the building, and upwards towards Luke's room. For a moment she thought that she saw his silhouette against the window, but she couldn't be certain. And, anyway, there was nothing that she could do. For the second time she had burned her boats. She strangled a sob and went round to the car park.

During the next weeks Merrill seemed to exist in limbo. She had no trouble in registering with a secretarial agency, and a variety of jobs carried her through the long, drab days. Common sense told her that by immersing herself in work the memory of the last months would recede, and with it would go her bitterness and sense of loss. After all, she rallied herself, she had got over Max, hadn't she? So why assume that the scars Luke had left on her would take longer to fade?

Yet when her salary cheque arrived she opened the envelope with trembling, hopeful fingers, and wept to find that the only other enclosure was a formal compliments slip from the accounts department.

Throughout the long evenings she worked in the

garden and planned what bulbs she would plant for spring flowers. Spring. . . Would it ever come again? And how empty it would seem, compared with the spring of this year when she had put the tall forsythia stems in the black glass vase in Luke's office.

Occasionally she went out with Diane from the neighbouring flat, and once made up a foursome with one of Diane's boyfriends and another man. It helped get her through one evening.

Sometimes, at the end of a busy day, she would tell herself that she was handling the situation well. But there were other moments when her guard was down, and she would see again her office at Woodline Design and wonder who was sitting at her desk now. Who was opening the mail with Luke? The memory of those sensitive hands, the clean square nails, the single white streak in his hair, would fill her mind with agony, and she would go on reading her book without taking in a word, or find herself deaf to the fact that the tape she was playing had long since finished.

She took up a late cancellation for a holiday and photographed the leaning tower of Pisa; in Florence sat drinking a cappuccino near the Piazza San Felice, thinking of those two English lovers, the Browning poets, who had lived there; threw a coin in the Trevi Fountain in Rome, wondering if she would ever come back. How wonderful it would be to explore these beautiful cities with Luke! In the hot August sunshine, among the strange, exciting smells, the vibrant colours, the centuries of history, Merrill's thoughts wandered randomly. Luke would know things about these places that the guide-books considered too unimportant to print; he would bring the ancient stones to life—as he had in Bruges.

And, once on that tack, she saw Luke everywhere:

in the purposeful stride of a man ahead of her in the crowd; in the dark, white-stranded head of a man bent over his newspaper; in a rich crimson and grey striped silk tie. . . Oh, was there no end to it? Would there *ever* be? What a long shadow he cast, reaching out to her even here!

Three days in Sorrento to unwind brought the holiday to a close, and then Merrill was home again, to be reminded of Rob's wedding by the engraved invitation that had arrived during her absence.

She fingered it with a sense of foreboding: Luke would be there, of course. Sufficient reason to plead an excuse. But she had promised Rob. . .and perhaps, after that final altercation in the office, Luke would keep his distance. Meanwhile she must buy something to wear. . .

By Saturday lunchtime Merrill was feeling very satisfied; the dress, with its big, softly pleated white collar, made a nothing of her waist, and its colour exactly matched the blue ribbon of the jaunty white boater she had found in an exclusive hat shop. There was nothing to go back to the flat for; the building would be empty, and here in the city centre she was, at least, among people.

The little French restaurant was dark after the sunlight outside, and as Merrill paused for a moment in the doorway, accustoming herself to the gloom, a voice called gaily, 'Merrill! Over here! Do join me.'

Merrill blinked, recognising Stella, and summoning up a quick smile. Heavens, if her heart beat like this at the sight of Luke's *stepmother*, how would it react when she came face to face again with *him*? she thought despairingly.

'Lovely to see you,' Stella was saying. She glanced at Merrill's bags. 'Out shopping?'

Merrill laughed. 'They're for Rob's wedding. . .'

'Oh, Rob's wedding.' Stella laughed too. 'You'd think there had never been a wedding before. . . You're looking wonderful, and what a gorgeous tan.'

Merrill was relieved to launch into a description of her holiday. Then unable to help herself, she said suddenly, 'How's Luke?'

'Working like ten men,' Stella answered disgustedly. 'He hasn't managed to find a replacement for you, so is having to make do with temporary staff. I was sorry to learn that you'd left.' She paused for a moment, then said delicately, 'You and Luke had a difference of opinion, I gather.'

'Something like that.' Merrill pushed the last morsel of caramelised orange around her plate. Her face felt pinched and bleak.

'What a pity,' Stella said thoughtfully, 'because— well, I felt that—— Still,' she resumed briskly, 'it's none of my business. Nevertheless, I *was* sorry about it, if only for Luke's sake. He's been marvellous to me, and particularly to Rob, despite the difference in their ages. A real brother. . . Have *you* any brothers, Merrill?'

Merrill shook her head. 'I haven't a living relation that I know of.'

'And I've only got Rob. And Luke, of course.' Stella smiled reflectively. 'I once had a brother, though—my twin.' She held out her wrist, and Merrill saw that from the heavy gold chain hung two small round lockets, each holding a tiny photograph. 'That was my second husband—Luke's and Rob's father,' Stella said, 'and this one here was my brother.'

Merrill leaned forward to look. 'He's very like Rob,' she remarked.

'Yes. We weren't identical twins, but we were very

close. I often thought Rob was like him in more than mere looks,' she went on thoughtfully, then her tone lightened. 'Well, now, shall we have coffee? Then I must dash. I'm still looking for shoes and bag for the wedding.'

As they left the restaurant, Stella said, 'We ought to do this again some time. We'll fix up something, shall we—at this famous wedding?'

'That would be lovely,' Merrill said automatically, hoping that Stella was merely being polite. After the wedding Merrill would try to let her acquaintance with Rob and Stella lapse for there was always the danger of meeting Luke again. And in her heart of hearts she knew that the sight of him, the sound of his voice, would demolish the wall she was trying to build to separate the present from the past.

September opened with high winds that sent the leaves scurrying along the pavements and brought decayed branches crashing down in Sherwood Forest.

On the first Saturday of the month Merrill's telephone rang, shrilling through the morning silence and making her jump. One aspect of her present way of life was the customary silence of the phone.

It was Simon Clifford, who lived next door to Bracken Cottage.

'Bad news, I'm afraid,' he warned. 'We had a gale last night, and it brought down some of the tiles on your cottage. The trouble is, Tom Wendell's away at a seminar.'

'I see.' Merrill thought rapidly. 'I'd better find a builder, then, and ask him to take a look.'

'We-ell, they're forecasting heavy rain,' Simon pointed out, 'but if I had a key to the cottage I could go in and fix up some temporary weatherproofing until the roof can be properly repaired.'

'I've got keys,' Merrill said quickly. 'I'll come straight over.'

She was dismayed to see that the damage was greater than she had expected. Bracken Cottage was old, and there was no felt beneath the red pantiles. With a good downpour it seemed probable that the bedroom ceiling below would come down.

Absently she noticed how neat it all was—quite different from the days when Elise lived there. Professor Wendell must be a very methodical man; he certainly wouldn't relish coming back to the chaos a fallen ceiling would create.

'It was good of you to get in touch with me, Simon,' she murmured as he hooked down the loft-ladder and she followed him up into the roof space.

'What are neighbours for?' he grunted. 'This heavy-duty polythene should do the trick if I can wedge it across the gaps.'

It was cold in the roof, with thin, sharp draughts blowing under the tiles, and Merrill hugged her arms about her as Simon wedged the polythene into place. She glanced around vaguely. She hadn't realised that Elise had used this space for storing things which weren't often needed. There were stacks of old art magazines, a broken easel, the white-painted bough which Elise had brought down at Christmas before trimming and hanging it over the inglenook fireplace. Merrill shivered, remembering the Christmas she had spent here after their parents died. How sad and desolate the cottage seemed now: empty—like a heart with no one to love.

Oh, really, she told herself crossly, you're becoming mawkish! But she would be relieved to get back to her own bright flat again, going about her normal Saturday chores.

She shivered again, glancing around, and saw a canvas propped against the gable wall, partly covered by a paint-daubed cloth. Moving gingerly, she went over to it and lifted one corner of the cloth, shining her torch on the canvas. Then swiftly she ripped the cloth aside.

A ragged tear ravaged the painted face that looked back at her. She gasped, then felt a pulse like a hammer-beat in her temple. The subject of the portrait was Rob; only it was a caricature of Rob—the eyes bluer than they were in real life, the mouth laughing, salacious, suggestive. . .and he wore a wide-brimmed black hat with a jaunty ostrich plume, and beneath his chin was a froth of lace. A cavalier. . .

CHAPTER TEN

MERRILL stood staring at the portrait, too stunned to deal with the battery of questions that bombed her brain.

'All done now.' Simon's cheerful voice made her jump. 'All right? Let's go.' He glanced at her then. 'Is something wrong? It *is* a bit claustrophobic up here.' Then his gaze moved down to the painting. 'Good heavens,' he said softly, squatting down to peer closely at the canvas, 'that's the—— What a pity it's damaged.' He stood up. 'Let's go down,' he said briskly. 'This has upset you—coming here and discovering some of Elise's work.'

Merrill found that she couldn't speak. Her teeth were chattering, and she felt chilled and perplexed. But a few moments later, in Simon's cottage, when he pulled up a chair to the fire and gently pressed her down into it, she managed to say, 'You—knew. . . The man in the portrait—you recognised him, didn't you?'

Simon poured a drop of rum into the two mugs of coffee he was making and handed one to Merrill. 'I recognised him, yes, but I never *knew* him. I don't think I even heard his name. He used to come to Elise's cottage.' Simon spoke carefully as if unsure of how his words would affect Merrill.

She cradled the warm mug gratefully in her cold hands. 'It's all right,' she told him, summoning up a tremulous smile. 'I *can* speak about Elise without falling to pieces now.' She took a sip of coffee. 'So he was—one of Elise's boyfriends?'

'Yes, I guess so. Yes, of course he was. Used to come for weekends. . . I never actually met him, but sometimes they would stretch out in the garden on warm days. I could hear them laughing and talking. They made quite a lot of noise.' He smiled reminiscently. 'They would call out to each other and——'

'But you said you never knew his name?' Merrill queried.

'Nor did I. Elise used to him "Lover" or "My lover", and he called her "Darling" or "Mistress" or other more—intimate names. There were times when I——'

But Merrill had stopped listening. Her mind, like a trap, had closed on that one word: lover. Could it be that. . .? Was it *possible* that those cryptic entries in Elise's diary referred to—*Rob*? That the initial 'L' meant 'Lover'? In short that 'L' meant Rob? Rob, and not *Luke*?

Unconsciously she drained her coffee, thanked Simon again and stood up. She needed to be alone to sort out the battery of questions, to *think*.

'You still look a little fragile,' Simon remarked. 'How about letting me take you out for a pub lunch? That'll fix you up.'

'No, I won't, but thank you, Simon. About the builder. . .' Merrill's voice trailed away. In her present state of mind it was almost beyond her capabilities to concentrate on practical matters.

'Oh, I know a man, and he's fairly local. I'll ask him to come first thing on Monday morning. I suppose the cottage *is* insured?'

'What?' With difficulty Merrill kept her thoughts away from the mystery of that portrait. 'Oh, yes—yes, it is. And again, Simon, thank you—for being such a good neighbour.'

There were questions that she was frantic to put to

him—about Elise, about Rob—but discretion and a sense of loyalty forbade them. But on the doorstep she paused, then said tentatively, 'Did—did Elise have many menfriends?'

'Quite a few. Well,' Simon smiled, 'she was rather gorgeous. It was only natural, unless a bloke was blind. I never made the running,' he added ruefully.

'This one—the one in the portrait. . .well, he looks rather young. Elise was almost thirty.'

'Mm, he was quite a bit younger than she was,' Simon said thoughtfully, snapping off a dead geranium head in the tub that flowered by his door. 'But that wouldn't have meant a thing to Elise, would it? Conventions didn't exist for her. She was a law unto herself and did what she wanted to do. One of your original free spirits, I guess. Well——' he shrugged '—she was your cousin; you knew her.'

'I wonder,' Merrill mused softly.

But Simon had heard. 'A valid point,' he remarked wryly. 'How much does anyone know—about anyone?' He glanced up at the sky. 'It's a good thing we got that roof seen to,' he said, then put out his palm as the first large drops of rain began to fall. 'I'll see the builder, then, and give you a ring on Monday evening to let you know what's happening. Drive carefully now.'

On the journey back into town Merrill deliberately froze out all thoughts of the past hour and its momentous revelation, concentrating instead on driving meticulously through the heavy rain. There would be time enough to examine this latest development when she got back. But subconsciously her mind was at work, and by the time she had garaged the car she was beginning to comprehend the appalling enormity of her mistake.

Once in the flat, she crouched by the window, staring

unseeingly out, her chin resting on clasped hands. So many questions assailed her that she couldn't think straight. Rob's party, and Richard Stirling's mention of Elise. . .and Luke's terse reply which effectively forbade further talk on the subject. Merrill frowned, then closed her eyes. Of course! Rob and Heather had just joined them then, and presumably Luke had felt that he had good reason for not wanting to prolong any conversation about Elise. After all, it was the occasion of Heather and Rob's engagement.

And all those other times when Luke had adroitly steered the conversation away from the topic of Elise. . . And she, Merrill, had jumped to the obvious conclusion that Luke was trying to hide his past association with her cousin because he felt some guilt over the manner of her death.

But it wasn't that way at all; it was *Rob*!

Oh, why on earth hadn't Luke told her that she had got it all wrong?

The answer came suddenly, a slap in the face that made her wince: because, on the only occasion when Merrill had actually confronted him with her suspicions—had brought them right out into the open—she hadn't given him a chance to explain. She had run from his office and away from Woodline Design.

The weekend was one of the most wretched she had ever known. Only one important factor emerged: she must apologise to Luke for misjudging him so. And yet a little misunderstanding still dogged her; why had Luke gone to such lengths to keep Rob's affair with Elise a secret? Would it have mattered so very much if Heather *had* found out about it? After all, it was only later that Rob had become serious about Heather.

Yes, she owed Luke an apology—not that he would care very much, considering his opinion of her. But for her own peace of mind she had to put matters straight. However, first she had to talk to Rob.

She telephoned him at lunchtime on Monday, and he seemed happy with her suggestion that they meet the following day. 'Not in the wine bar, though,' she insisted hastily; she couldn't take a chance on Luke walking in. 'Let's try that little Italian place—the Astra.'

Over spaghetti they chatted casually for a while, then Rob said, 'You're looking thinner. Must be a bug; Luke's got it, too, not to mention behaving like a bear with a sore head when I told him I wanted to take an early lunch.'

'You didn't tell him you were meeting me, though?' Merrill said, alarmed.

'Not likely! He never exactly encouraged our friendship. When I got back from Maslins' that day and wanted to know where you were, he clammed up on me.' Rob glanced at her curiously. 'What happened? Did you have a blazing row or something?'

'You could say that. It wasn't very pleasant.' Merrill recalled Luke's baffled expression when she'd accused him of being involved with Elise, and felt her body grow hot with shame. She put down her fork, and after a moment said, 'Rob, how well did you know my cousin—Elise Masters?'

Rob looked up, his blue eyes startled, then he gave a low whistle. 'Elise was your cousin? I had no idea! Luke told me that she died in a car accident some time ago. I'm sorry. . .I didn't know that you were related to her.'

Merrill, watching him closely, saw nothing in his expression except genuine regret and concern.

'You didn't answer my question, Rob,' she reminded him quietly.

For a moment he toyed with his fork. 'How do you know that I knew Elise?' he asked in a low voice.

'I learned from her diary that she had been seeing quite a lot of—of a man. But I didn't know who that man was—until I found a portrait she had painted of you.'

'That cavalier thing?' Rob looked embarrassed. 'We were fooling about. . .' His voice died for a moment. 'Oh, hell,' he muttered, 'must we go into it?'

'Please.' Merrill touched his hand imploringly. 'It's important to me. Just how well *did* you know her?'

For a moment Merrill thought that Rob wasn't going to answer, then he sighed, loosened the knot of his tie, and said, 'I don't know what all this is about, but I can see that it does matter to you. Well, I suppose you'd say that Elise and I had a very close relationship for a time.' He paused again, maddeningly, Merrill thought, twisting spaghetti around his fork. 'We met at a party. I'd been going out with Heather on and off, with one or two other girls in between. Nothing serious, no commitment or anything like that. Then I saw Elise and—wham! She was. . .' He made a helpless gesture. 'She was wearing a red dress. She looked like a Spanish gypsy—exotic, vivid, volatile. I recall that she made all the other women at the party look drab, washed-out.'

Merrill nodded; she knew exactly what Rob meant.

'When she put out a few signals that she—well, fancied me, you can guess how I felt. Ten feet tall.' He pushed his half-eaten meal away from him.

'Go on,' Merrill prompted.

Rob gave her an embarrassed scowl. 'What can I say? That was the start of an affair. A sizzling affair. Elise was—oh, I don't know—*different*. She wasn't interested in security, a home and family, permanency. She knew exactly what she wanted, and she had got it—the only kind of life that would keep her happy. She was totally in charge of herself.' He smoothed his jaw thoughtfully. 'But she was fun—immense fun. Exciting to be with. . . She was a fair bit older than me, but that was no problem. Age simply didn't come into the kind of relationship we had. If she'd been forty, I doubt if it would have made any difference— to either of us.'

'You were—in love with her?' Merrill said gently.

'Love?' Rob scowled again. 'I simply don't know! I was besotted with her. There was this tremendous *pull*, a fascination. . .' He shook his head helplessly.

'Yet in the end you dropped her,' Merrill pursued.

Rob's eyebrows shot up. 'I didn't. What on earth gave you that idea? It was the reverse.'

'Oh, but——' Merrill thought of the ruined portrait, the damage which she had assumed had been deliberately inflicted by Elise in a mood of despair. Had she got *that* wrong too?

Rob stared at a space above Merrill's head. 'I arrived at her cottage one Friday evening, expecting to spend the weekend with her. And along with the meal she served up my notice. Told me it was over.' He sat back as the waiter brought coffee. 'I was angry—who wouldn't be? Well, just dropping it on me like that, right out of the blue. I had absolutely no idea that she was intending to end everything between us.'

He fell silent for a few moments, shredding the paper that had wrapped his sugar cube.

'You *are* telling me the truth, Rob? I mean—that Elise ended it?'

'Sure I am,' he said, aggrieved. 'She—laughed at me. She reminded me that we both knew the deal—no strings. That we owed each other nothing.' He sighed. 'All the old clichés: it was good while it lasted, and so on. It was true, of course. That was how we'd set it up from the beginning. Only I would have liked it to last a bit longer,' he added softly.

Merrill was still trying to come to terms with this reversal of her convictions. Elise, and not Rob, had finished the affair, so where did that leave her suspicions about Elise's death? 'Why did she finish with you?' she asked after a moment. 'Was there another man?' It seemed clear now that there was a side to Elise which Merrill hadn't known at all.

'No.' Rob shook his head. 'It was work. She felt that I was getting in the way. She said that she didn't want any diversions because she was about to start something big, something that really fired her up. Oh, I was too shattered and angry to take much notice—a series of paintings with a common theme—medieval music, I think. Oh, *I* don't know,' he added irritably. 'As I said, I wasn't in the mood to listen to details.'

For a moment they were both silent, Merrill recalling the portfolio of preliminary sketches she had found among Elise's effects.

'The thing about Elise,' Rob resumed succinctly, 'was that she never did anything by halves. You should know that, being her cousin. She gave one hundred and one per cent of herself to whatever was important at the time.' He sighed, then went on reflectively, 'In the end we parted amicably. I couldn't blame her; she'd laid things on the line from the start, as I had. As a matter of fact, before I left on that Friday evening I bought a painting from her—*The Blind Gypsy*—for my mother's birthday.'

With a piercing stab of remorse at yet another misconstruction, Merrill recalled the painting she had thought belonged to Luke, which hung on the wall outside his room.

'There,' Rob said decisively. 'I think I've answered your question fully. And now, suppose you tell me why you wanted to know all this?'

'That's fair enough, I guess,' Merrill said slowly. 'I knew that Elise was seeing a lot of *someone*. I also knew that soon after she stopped seeing him she died. An accident, they said. But Elise was a first-class driver.' She paused for a moment. 'I began to wonder—to suspect—that she had deliberately crashed her car because this man—*you*—had walked out on her. That she'd been really and truly in love and couldn't go on. Going through her diary, as I had to, seemed somehow—obscene. Maybe I was in no state to think straight at that time, and I got it into my head that. . .' Her voice faltered into silence as she was swamped by the ramifications of the whole distorted story which she had put together. She couldn't have been more wrong—about everything!

Rob's hand covered hers with comforting warmth. 'And you thought I had broken her heart?' he said softly. 'Oh, Merrill, why on earth didn't you get all this off your chest earlier?'

'Because I only found the portrait—I was only able to identify the man in her diary when I had to go out to the cottage last Saturday. You see, Rob, she didn't use your name in her diary entries.'

'That figures,' he nodded. 'She didn't use it when we were together either. That was all part of it. It was purely a fun situation between us. Oh, I don't mean to sound flippant,' he said quickly. 'I think I'll always be grateful for those few weeks when Elise and I were together. I was lucky to have her, to have that kind of—well, enchantment, I suppose.'

They were both quiet for a while, then Merrill said, 'And Luke—he knew about you and Elise? You once said something about him warning you away from magic?'

Rob nodded. 'He met her soon after I did. She wanted us to make her a Shaker-style chest, and there was something a bit peculiar about the dimensions, so Luke and I went to Bracken Cottage. Luke's no fool; he could see that so far as I was concerned Elise was more than just a client. Later, when Luke and I had a trip north, we delivered the chest on the way. Well,' he grinned, 'when Elise wanted a thing she wanted it *now*. In the event, she let something slip, and Luke's suspicions were confirmed.'

'He didn't like her?' Merrill pressed.

Rob shook his head. 'I don't know. Probably not. At any rate, he disapproved, but perhaps that was partly for my mother's sake.' In answer to Merrill's questioning face, he went on, 'I think I once told you that I'd been a bit—wild. I'd given Luke and Ma a few problems. I got mixed up with the wrong crowd for a while. . . Oh, Luke saw to it that I got out before there was any real harm done, but. . .' His voice died away.

'Go on,' Merrill prompted.

'Well, I'm not sure that I should be raking up all this, but in a way it *is* related to Luke's attitude towards Elise, and you *did* ask. . . My mother had a twin brother. She thought the world of him. But he was a bit of a womaniser and got mixed up in some scandal; I never knew the whole story. Anyway, he left the country. He had a boat and used to charter trips in the Mediterranean. I don't know if he was also running contraband, or what, but I think there was something shady about it. He died at sea.'

'How dreadful for your mother,' Merrill said softly, recalling the little locket which Stella had shown her.

'Yes. Well, it seems that I resemble him—physically, anyway. Maybe in other ways, too. And I guess my mother thought I might go the same way. As I said, there'd been plenty of women in Uncle Paul's life. I don't know, but it might be that Luke thought Elise would turn out to be one of my problems—a bad influence on me. So he was very wary of her, to say the least.'

Rob brightened suddenly. 'But now,' he said cheerfully, 'all that's in the past. Ma and Luke are relieved to see that I'm settling down at last. And they both think the world of Heather. She's right for me. And at last I've learned that, too.'

Merrill nodded. 'You *both* seem right together,' she agreed, glancing at her watch. 'Good heavens, I've got to get back— It's been quite a lunch, Rob. Thanks for being so honest with me. You've cleared up quite a lot of questions that were haunting me.'

'You'll keep all this between the two of us,' Rob said anxiously. 'I mean—well, I've been no worse than plenty of other guys, but anyway it's—irrelevant now.'

'Yes, of course it is. Don't worry; you can trust me.' Merrill smiled. 'Well, see you in church, as they say.'

'You bet. I'll be there with bells—as they say,' Rob laughed. 'Wedding bells.'

How strange, Merrill reflected that evening, as her mind did a re-run of the lunchtime conversation, that she hadn't felt at all bitter towards Rob when, on Saturday, she had learned that *he* had been the man in question. Everything she had thrown in Luke's direction should have been transferred to Rob, really. Yet that hadn't been the case. But perhaps, on second thoughts, it wasn't so strange: Luke was special, unique. Couldn't it be that she had needed to loathe him so that she could smother the awakening of her real feelings for him? He'd been important enough to warrant a strong, positive reaction, whereas Rob was just a pleasant friend, but nothing really special.

If only she had realised, on that first morning when she had seen Luke crossing the reception area of Woodline Design, that he would make such a shattering impact upon her, then she might have walked away. But instead she had stayed. And she had let his kisses melt her, let his touch arouse her, his anger scorch her; small, tender gestures had somehow reached her, frail as dandelion seeds, but becoming strongly rooted, to survive somehow in the bitter darkness of her rejection of him. One way and another Luke had filled her life. And he still filled it, but now it could only be with regret for the enormity of her mistakes.

The wedding day dawned in perfect September weather. A thin, silky mist hung over the city, reminding Merrill of the water-colour townscapes which, in her gentler moods, Elise had painted so well. But by ten o'clock the mist had gone, burned off by the sun which shone from a clear blue sky.

Merrill dressed with care. A little of her warm Italian tan remained, but inside she felt cold and nervous. She hadn't seen Luke since the afternoon when she'd run from the office, having confined her windsurfing to early Saturday mornings, safe in the knowledge that his tuition of the children took place later in the day.

His manner as he greeted her at the church door, then ushered her to her seat, did nothing to dispel her apprehension. Rather, after that first heart-clenching moment when she saw him—so tall, so incredibly right in formal dress—she felt more wretched than ever: he was merely as courteous as the occasion demanded.

For Merrill the marriage service was a kaleidoscope

of images seen at a distance because of her acute consciousness of Luke's presence. Rob, debonair and well-groomed; the sunlight through stained glass making a coloured mosaic on the stone floor; the music swelling as Heather, in ivory lace, arrived on her father's arm, and Rob turning quickly to look at her, then watching her all the way down the aisle as she came towards him; the hot prick of tears in Merrill's eyes at the beautiful solemnity of the ceremony.

Even afterwards at Four Winds, where a marquee had been set up on the lawn, and the guests mingled, Merrill still saw the affair as a disjointed series of impressions. Champagne. . .toasts. . .speeches—some witty, others sentimental. . . And beneath it all her agony of eargerness to speak to Luke alone battling with her growing apprehension. After all, why should her apology be important—to *him*?

But he was elusive, and she could only fill the long minutes with a pretence of animation as she was absorbed into a group of Heather's relations, something inside her dying by the second as time passed and Luke kept his distance.

Heather had changed into a raspberry-coloured linen suit, and she and Rob circulated, saying goodbye to their guests. When they reached Merrill Heather said, 'When we get back you will come and see us, won't you? We've got a super apartment near the marina. I'm longing to show it off to everyone.'

Merrill smiled at the glowing face and said, 'Yes, I'd love to see it. . .' But it wasn't true; today the invisible hand of fate seemed to be drawing a thick black line under that particular chapter of her life which involved anything related to Luke.

The bride and groom left, and people began to drift away. It was all over now, this ordeal which Merrill had anticipated with hope and dread. It was patently obvious that she wasn't going to get an opportunity to speak to Luke; it seemed possible that he had manipulated that.

And suddenly she couldn't escape quickly enough. She was stunned by a sense of defeat and disappointment which only emphasised how important her intentions had really been. And now the effort of hiding that failure was too much to bear here in the sunlit garden. She went towards the house to say goodbye to Stella, and as she turned the corner of the building she almost collided with Luke. For a moment she stared at him, then quickly, before she lost courage, she said, 'Luke. . .I have to talk to you——'

'Won't it keep?' he said, raising an eyebrow. 'Right now I have my hands full.'

His words hit her like a sudden icy shower, and her self-control snapped at last. 'The same old Luke,' she whispered despairingly, 'as rude as ever.'

'Not rude,' he said quietly, 'merely straight. Which is more than you ever were with me—until, of course, that last day at the office when you took the lid off and let it all boil over—all the things that had been bugging you.'

'You're right,' she muttered after a moment. 'And I'm sorry—about everything.' She stared down at her toe drawing patterns on the paving. 'That's what I wanted to talk about,' she added in a whisper.

He watched her face thoughtfully for a moment. 'Look, I'm trying to sort out some transport for a couple of guests. Here——' he put a glass of champagne into her hand '—go into my study—along the small corridor—and wait for me there.'

The book-lined room with its trophies and framed photographs was cool and dim, but Merrill's feelings left no space for interest in her surroundings. She took a sip of champagne then put the glass down. It tasted of nothing. If Luke didn't come soon she would lose her nerve altogether and bolt. He could be so—daunting.

Then he came in, and she sat down quickly. 'So,' he prompted softly, 'you want to talk.'

Merrill nodded. 'I—I know everything now,' she murmured.

He watched her guardedly for a moment, then he said, 'Do I take it that you're referring to Elise?'

Merrill nodded dumbly, ashamed of the tears which blinded her suddenly. A result of all the strain she'd been through, she thought distractedly, groping for her handkerchief.

'Here,' he said, 'take mine. . .' Then, in a strangled tone, 'Don't cry, Merrill. I don't think I could cope with the memory of you sitting in my study weeping.'

She sniffed a little, and dabbed her eyes. 'I don't know what came over me.' She gave a watery, apologetic smile. 'Weddings can be. . .' She stopped suddenly and gazed at him. 'Why should you bother to remember me at all—except unpleasantly?' she murmured.

'Because,' he said a little bitterly, 'you're—unforgettable. I told you that once before.' His mouth twisted as if in self-mockery.

'I remember,' she whispered. 'After Bruges. Oh, Luke,' she went on brokenly, shaking her head. 'Luke. . . But let me talk,' she said quickly. 'Let me say what I came to say before my nerve goes. I made so many mistakes about you. And about Elise. And I encouraged you to make mistakes about me, too. Somehow it seemed safer that way.' She hesitated, then went on in a small voice, 'I think I was afraid of what you could do to me. I dared not—let you *in*. You see, I thought I had evidence that you and Elise had had an affair, even though you wouldn't admit it. And I believed that the affair might have had something to do with her death. So it seemed better that you should go on thinking that I was just——'

'Out for a good time? That you had strings of boyfriends?' he put in.

'Yes. Do you remember that evening—I hadn't been working for you for very long—and you gave me a lift home?' As he nodded she went on, 'I'd had a bit of a knock in—in a relationship with a man in London, and I was very miserable over Elise's death. The last thing I needed at that time was pity. I didn't want you to think I was—feeble, having trouble in relocating myself, in getting things together again. So I suppose I led you into thinking the exact opposite—that I had a swinging social life.'

'I see.' Luke nodded slowly, his gaze never moving from her face. 'And so, of course, I jumped to the obvious conclusion in Bruges when you met Richard.'

'Yes, and I let you. It was my—my refuge. I couldn't let you get close because, as I said, I suspected that you were implicated in Elise's death.'

'You mean the accident?' He frowned. 'You once said something about Elise's frame of mind, and I didn't quite see what you were implying. But, leaving that aside for a moment, during our—association— you made veiled insinuations about me and Elise——'

'I know. And I was wrong. It wasn't you at all. Oh, I can't go into all the details now—I've lived with them, and with my remorse ever since I learned that— it wasn't you, it was Rob.'

'Have you been talking to him?' Luke asked quietly.

'Yes. I asked him to meet me when I found out proof that he——'

'Look, can't we leave it now?' Luke interrupted gently. 'It was between Elise and Rob. It was their affair, and it ended a long time ago. Rob's married now; Elise, unfortunately, died in an accident. Can't we put it all behind us?'

Merrill shook her head. 'I've *got* to talk it through, don't you see?' She raised a furtive finger to brush away a tear that still hung on her lashes. 'Oh, Luke,' she cried, 'why didn't *you* tell me I was wrong? On the day I left Woodline you *knew* that I'd made an enormous mistake, yet you——'

'I might have tried,' he said in a low voice, 'but you didn't want to listen. And also I couldn't do something that might jeopardise Rob's marriage to Heather.' As Merrill looked at him questioningly, he went on, 'Knowing, by then, just how you felt about the circumstances of Elise's death, you could have done a lot of damage.'

'I thought that—wondered if it was—suicide because of this man she'd been seeing,' Merrill said in a small voice.

'That's a hell of a burden to have carried around with you all this time,' Luke said feelingly. He got up and moved across to the bookshelves, then turned to face Merrill. The light from the window struck his face and she noticed small lines which she didn't remember, an increased leanness emphasising the strong bone-structure of his cheeks and jaw.

'There was also Stella to think of,' Luke resumed. 'She's had a lot of knocks in her life, although you might not think it to look at her, perhaps. A much-loved brother dying in rather questionable circumstances, then her first husband. . .and then having to nurse her second husband—my father—through a long illness at a time when she herself wasn't well. And the cruise she was on at that time—well, that was to convalesce after a very serious operation, although,' he added wryly, 'she would probably kill me for mentioning it. So you do see, don't you, that I felt my hands were tied?'

Merrill nodded silently. 'I seem to have made an awful mess of things,' she murmured.

Luke smiled suddenly. 'Nothing that can't be remedied,' he said softly. 'So to continue: just when everything seemed to be going right—Rob settling down and getting serious over Heather, and Stella recovering—you came along. And on the very morning that I learned of Elise's death you'll remember that Rob walked into the office, back from his holiday. As I said, you could have upset the apple cart badly. I was determined that Stella's newly found peace of mind wouldn't be disturbed.'

Merrill nodded. 'I understand.'

'Do you? I wonder. . .' Luke watched her for a moment in silence, and Merrill's gaze fell. 'You see, Merrill, I had two reasons for wanting to keep you and Rob apart.'

'I don't quite follow.' Merrill looked at him, her eyes wide, clouded by confusion.

'Two reasons,' he repeated. 'The first one being that I had put two and two together from your various veiled remarks, and I suspected that you knew about Rob's relationship with Elise and that you were, in a sense, gunning for him. Of course,' he added with a twisted smile, 'it wasn't until your last day in the office that I realised you were under the impression that it was *I* who'd had the affair with Elise.'

Merrill nodded miserably. 'And I didn't give you the

chance to put things straight,' she murmured. 'But you said *two* reasons. . .?'

Absently Luke took the carnation from his button-hole and dropped it on the bookshelves. He nodded. 'The second reason was that you, too, have an impact that can be quite devastating. Oh, yes,' he went on, 'that's no exaggeration. And, knowing Rob's past propensity for attractive women—well. . .' he shrugged '. . .need I say more?'

For a moment they were both silent, then Merrill said softly, 'I was never, at any time, in the least attracted to Rob, you know. I like him, but that's all.'

'I realise that now,' Luke said heavily. 'But it didn't help matters when, that evening in your flat, you did your damnedest—and succeeded—in sounding like a hard-hearted go-getter, so it became even more important to steer him away. Of course, I'd overlooked one thing. . .' His voice faded.

'Oh, I wish I'd known about Elise and Rob.' Merrill beat her hands together, her expression anguished. 'Your—your integrity cost me an awful lot of misery,' she whispered.

For a moment he looked savage. 'And what the hell did you think it did to me? You hated me!'

'I was afraid *not* to. . .' Merrill's voice faded into silence. Then she breathed, 'You see, I had to—to put all my energies into hating you because—because——' She couldn't go on.

Luke shot her a strange, enquiring glance, then he bent, reaching for her glass. 'This champagne's *warm*,' he said disgustedly. 'I'll get us both a fresh glass.'

He went out, and Merrill sensed that he was giving her a breathing space. Perhaps he, too, needed one. The emotions of the last minutes had drained her. But it was what she had wanted. She sat back, closing her

eyes, incapable of coherent thought, and then, so
slowly that she found herself holding her breath, a tiny
spark kindled inside: they had talked through a tangle
of mistakes, yet somewhere in it there was something
else. An occasional phrase, a glance. . .clues that were
not at all tangled.

When Luke came back with fresh glasses, he sat on
the arm of her chair. 'Feeling better?' he said softly, a
slight smile lifting his mouth. She answered the smile,
nodding. 'My poor, mixed-up Merrill,' he whispered.
'You must have gone through hell. But you didn't go
alone. You put me through it, too. You had me
imprisoned by your loathing—most of the time. But
there were other moments, too. Yet every time I
thought I'd broken out of that cage you pushed me
back again.'

'I know. I had to. I was trying to solve a mystery,
and you were my prime suspect. I had to keep reminding myself of that because——'

'Yes?' he whispered. 'Because—what?'

She couldn't answer, but her eyes spoke for her.

Then Luke got up again, restlessly. 'And—Richard?'
he asked roughly, his back towards her.

'*Richard*?' Brought suddenly back to a world of
misunderstandings, she stared at his broad shoulders in
dismay.

'His car was outside your flat very early on the
morning after Rob's engagement party,' Luke
reminded her.

'And you thought we had spent the night together?'
Merrill shook her head slowly. 'He drove me home
that night. He came up for coffee, then his car wouldn't
start. He had to leave it, so he borrowed mine to get
back to his hotel. He's somewhere in Essex now, I

think. I don't know. He just happened to be in this area on the night of Rob's party. That's all.'

Luke turned then and smiled. Those small new lines she had noticed were gone from his face. 'So I owe you an apology; I misjudged you, too. But let's forget that the word sorry even exists.' He took her glass from her and set it on the top of the bookshelves, then he said softly, 'You look somehow—different.'

'I expect it's the hat.'

'Mmm. Could be. I don't think so, though.' He put out his hands and lifted off the little straw boater and laid it down. Then she felt his fingers in her hair, teasing out the curls into her usual hairstyle. 'No,' he murmured, his gaze moving over her face and lingering on each feature. 'It wasn't the hat. It's *you*. You look as if you're not haunted any longer; there's a strange quality of—of repose about you. I've never seen it before, not even in those few moments that stayed so vividly in my memory. And it's beautiful.' He held out his hands. 'Get up,' he said softly. 'I'll show you why.'

Wondering, Merrill stood up, and Luke slipped into the chair, drawing her down on to his knees and putting his arms around her. She wondered distractedly if he could feel the mad racing of her heart.

For a moment he held her closely in a silence that spoke more clearly than words, telling her that all the friction was over, all the pain. . . 'There's just one thing more, darling,' he said at last. 'Are you satisfied now that Elise's death *was* an accident?'

Still bemused by Luke's closeness and the responses tingling through her veins, Merrill nodded. 'She had an exciting project on her mind. Maybe she lost concentration for a moment——'

'And that's all it takes, unfortunately.' Somewhere in the house a clock chimed. 'Four o'clock,' Luke murmured huskily, 'and it's the damnedest time to say what I want to say—what I've wanted to say many times. . . There ought to be moonlight, starlight or sunset, music—— But I shall say it anyhow.' He took her chin between finger and thumb, turning her face and drowning her in the warm amber light of his eyes. 'I love you. You came into my life bringing something I had never known before. But you made me fight it, and I did. Yet, whatever the time, whatever the day, I wanted to—kiss you,' he breathed against her lips. 'To kiss you, hold you, and go on and on. . . To make love to you simply because—I had fallen in love with you.'

The words and his tone lit a glorious fire in Merrill's blood that consumed the weeks of misery and suspicion as if they had never been. And his kiss when it came had a new depth and intensity born of the freedom they had both found during the past moments. She put her hands up to his head, felt the thick hair beneath her fingers, and the rekindled flame leapt in every part of her body.

He drew away slowly, reluctantly, looking down at her trembling lips, her wide, smoky eyes. 'How right I was,' she whispered, 'to be afraid of what you could do to me.'

'And are you afraid now?' he breathed.

'No.' She smiled at him, her eyes returning the love she saw in his face. 'I welcome it.'

'Then come back to me. I want to marry you.'

Merrill's eyes widened. In her wildest dreams she hadn't imagined that Rob's wedding day would bring *this*! The most she had hoped for was a shedding of the burden of guilt she had carried, and Luke's understanding.

And now it seemed that she had his understanding—

and his love. She wanted to weep again, but this time with joy.

'I want you to marry me,' Luke said, giving her a little shake. 'Don't be so obtuse, darling. And don't say this is so sudden. It's not, you know. It's been on my mind since Bruges.'

He kissed her again, his lips lingering on hers as if they had all the time in the world. Dimly Merrill heard a car door bang outside, then a motor started up. 'But first,' Luke resumed, 'before we get married, we've got some living to do, time to make up—hours, days, weeks to share. Will you, darling? There's so much that we——'

He broke off, grimacing, as Stella's voice called, 'Luke? Where are you? Is Merrill with you? Tom's taking me into town, and I wondered if she'd like a lift.'

Luke raised enquiring eyebrows at Merrill. 'Now's your chance,' he murmured. 'Well, *would* you like a lift?'

Merrill touched his mouth with her fingertips. 'What do you think?' she whispered.

Luke held her tightly against him. '*I* think I'm even happier than Rob,' he breathed. Then, raising his voice a little, 'No lift, thank you, Stella. Merrill's staying.' As he spoke Merrill felt his heartbeat against her own.

Yes, she thought before she drew his face down to hers again, I *am* staying—staying in the only place for me: Luke's heart.

PENNY JORDAN

A
COLLECTION

Volume 2

From the bestselling author of *Power Play*, *The Hidden Years* and *Lingering Shadows* comes a second collection of three sensuous love stories, beautifully presented in one special volume.

Featuring:

FIRE WITH FIRE
CAPABLE OF FEELING
SUBSTITUTE LOVER

Available from May 1993   Priced: £4.99

W❂RLDWIDE

Accept 4 FREE Romances and 2 FREE gifts

FROM READER SERVICE

An irresistible invitation from Mills & Boon Reader Service. Please accept our offer of 4 free Romances, a CUDDLY TEDDY and a special MYSTERY GIFT... Then, if you choose, go on to enjoy 6 captivating Romances every month for just £1.70 each, postage and packing free. Plus our FREE Newsletter with author news, competitions and much more.

**Send the coupon below to:
Reader Service, FREEPOST,
PO Box 236, Croydon,
Surrey CR9 9EL.**

NO STAMP REQUIRED

Yes! Please rush me 4 Free Romances and 2 free gifts!
Please also reserve me a Reader Service Subscription. If I decide to subscribe I can look forward to receiving 6 brand new Romances each month for just £10.20, post and packing free.
If I choose not to subscribe I shall write to you within 10 days - I can keep the books and gifts whatever I decide. I may cancel or suspend my subscription at any time. I am over 18 years of age.

Ms/Mrs/Miss/Mr ———————————————————————— EP30R

Address ————————————————————————————————

Postcode———————— Signature ————————————

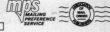

Next Month's Romances

Each month you can choose from a wide variety of romance with Mills & Boon. Below are the new titles to look out for next month, why not ask either Mills & Boon Reader Service or your Newsagent to reserve you a copy of the titles you want to buy — just tick the titles you would like and either post to Reader Service or take it to any Newsagent and ask them to order your books.

Please save me the following titles:		Please tick	√
HIGH RISK	Emma Darcy		
PAGAN SURRENDER	Robyn Donald		
YESTERDAY'S ECHOES	Penny Jordan		
PASSIONATE CAPTIVITY	Patricia Wilson		
LOVE OF MY HEART	Emma Richmond		
RELATIVE VALUES	Jessica Steele		
TRAIL OF LOVE	Amanda Browning		
THE SPANISH CONNECTION	Kay Thorpe		
SOMETHING MISSING	Kate Walker		
SOUTHERN PASSIONS	Sara Wood		
FORGIVE AND FORGET	Elizabeth Barnes		
YESTERDAY'S DREAMS	Margaret Mayo		
STORM OF PASSION	Jenny Cartwright		
MIDNIGHT STRANGER	Jessica Marchant		
WILDER'S WILDERNESS	Miriam Macgregor		
ONLY TWO CAN SHARE	Annabel Murray		

If you would like to order these books in addition to your regular subscription from Mills & Boon Reader Service please send £1.80 per title to: Mills & Boon Reader Service, Freepost, P.O. Box 236, Croydon, Surrey, CR9 9EL, quote your Subscriber No:..................................... (If applicable) and complete the name and address details below. Alternatively, these books are available from many local Newsagents including W.H.Smith, J.Menzies, Martins and other paperback stockists from 14th May 1993.

Name:..

Address:..

....Post Code:...........................

To Retailer: If you would like to stock M&B books please contact your regular book/magazine wholesaler for details.

You may be mailed with offers from other reputable companies as a result of this application. If you would rather not take advantage of these opportunities please tick box ☐